The Destroyer

MISSING LINK #39

by Warren Murphy

PINNACLE BOOKS LOS ANGELES

DESTROYER #39: MISSING LINK

Copyright © 1980 by Richard Sapir and Warren Murphy

An original Pinnacle Books edition, published for the first time anywhere.

First printing, February 1980
Second printing, September 1980

ISBN: 0-523-41254-1

Cover llustration by Hector Garrido

Printed in the United States of America

PINNACLE BOOKS, INC.
2029 Century Park East
Los Angeles, California 90067

Missing Link

CHAPTER ONE

Bobby Jack Billings had gone to bed deciding that the next day he would change his drinking habits. Not that drinking was a problem. Beer drinkers never had real drinking problems. He had read that in the *Hills Gazette* or someplace. Beer drinkers never got falling-down drunk, running their cars over school kids, stealing and cheating to get enough money to support their habit. No. That was whiskey drinkers. Bobby Jack was a beer drinker and didn't have that kind of problem.

That thought gave him enough solace to fall asleep, so he drained the last few drops from his can of beer and dropped the empty on the floor next to the bed. As he was nodding off, he carefully devised his drinking schedule for the next day. He would not have a beer before breakfast. In fact, he would not have any beer before lunchtime. Maybe after work in the afternoon he might have a couple, and maybe one or two with supper, and perhaps one, late at night, just to relieve the day's tensions. But that was all.

When he woke up he had a throbbing headache.

His mouth tasted like a testing center for Q Tips. The back of his throat burned hot enough to ignite the cotton. He had trouble finding his eyeglasses.

He splashed water on his face and then tried to open his eyes wide. It made the day seem a little more bearable, but the headache persisted. He remembered having lain in bed the night before, making some major decision, but in the iron light of morning he couldn't remember what the decision was. Perhaps he could remember it after he had a beer.

He padded barefoot out to the kitchen, a soft-bodied man with a soft face, and pulled a can from the refrigerator. The can began to sweat in his hand immediately, because of the great difference in temperature between the kitchen in the hot American South and the refrigerator, which he kept turned to its lowest cooling level. This was murderous on iceberg lettuce, filling its watery bulk with ice crystals that turned the lettuce to mush when it thawed, but he liked his beer cold and he didn't eat all that much lettuce anyway, so it was a small price to pay.

He popped off the easy-open top and cut his right index finger. He poured beer over it. Another good thing about beer. It was a natural antiseptic.

He drank the can in two large rollicking swallows. He still could not remember what he had been thinking about the night before but, praise be heaven, the headache was going away, and maybe just another dose of the same medicine. . . .

He drank the second can more slowly and halfway through the pains in his head vanished, and he remembered he had been thinking about cutting

3

down on his beer drinking. It seemed like a very good idea, but it was too late to worry about today. He would start his new program of restraint tomorrow.

He finished the second can and went to the bathroom. His eyes worked better now and he examined his face and decided there really wasn't any need to shave. He had shaved yesterday and anyway everybody in the family was blessed with light beards. You could hardly notice any stubble. His father had sometimes gone three or four days without shaving and no one ever complained. He used his fingers as a comb to push his sandy hair back from his round face. He bent his head down toward his right armpit and when he survived the tentative inhalation, he decided he could get through the day without a shower. Or at least the morning. He would probably take a shower in the afternoon, but that was something to think about later.

He emptied his bladder. He remembered telling reporters once that nobody buys beer, they only rent it, and they had all printed it and no one had seemed to notice that he had stolen the line from Archie Bunker on television. That was a long time ago, though, when the reporters weren't always getting on him about something. But what could you expect from a liberal Jewish conspiracy? Thousands of reporters, all liberals, all Jews, and not one of them drank beer. They drank brandy, for crying out loud. Or cream sherry. Fag drinkers. A fag, liberal, Jewish conspiracy.

Back in the kitchen, he took out another beer

and, on a whim, looked to see if there was any food.

There was a Slim Jim smoked sausage in a cellophane wrapper and there was an egg on the rack. Good. A hard-boiled egg and a sausage. A man's breakfast.

He cracked the egg on the edge of the counter. The gooey yolk and slimy white ran onto the counter.

"Craps," he hissed. Bobby Jack jumped back so that the egg didn't drip on his bare feet. He thought it had been hard-boiled. He remembered boiling some eggs just a day or so ago. Or maybe it was a week.

He held the Slim Jim in his other hand. Well, tomorrow he would eat that because you couldn't eat a saloon sausage without an egg and there were no more eggs in the house.

He took out another beer and counted the remaining cans. Only a dozen. He'd have more delivered. He slammed the refrigerator door shut. He opened the can and took a swallow. As he leaned forward to toss the pop-top toward the garbage can, he stepped into the raw egg which had slimed its way to the floor.

"Craps," he said. He could see it was going to be another one of those days.

He walked toward the front door with the beer can in his hand. The *New York Times* was just inside the front door. He should read it, he knew. At least glance at its editorial page. But who cared? He knew what it would say. It would criticize him, criticize the Arabs, criticize his brother-in-law, praise the Jews and come out for abortion and against capital punishment, and frankly the *New York Times* was getting to be a pain in the ass. What could you expect from a newspaper that was a tool of the international Zionist conspiracy?

He kicked the paper aside, then wiped his eggy foot on it. He opened the door and walked out onto the front porch. The two regular Secret Service men were sitting there.

"Hi, boys," he said. "Want a beer?" He waved the can at the two men in business suits. They shook their heads.

On the dirt walkway leading up to the porch were three people carrying pads and ball-point pens. One of them yelled to him.

"Mr. Billings, last night, the National Jewish Alliance voted to censure you for your statements. What do you think of that?"

"They can kiss my ass," he yelled back. Who the hell was the National Jewish Alliance? He would have said more but the two Secret Service men had risen from their wooden chairs and were standing in front of him.

"What's the matter?" he said.

"Bobby Jack," said the older of the two. "You'd better go put on your pants before you hold a press conference."

Bobby Jack Billings looked down. He was wearing only his skivvies and a stained tee shirt. He chuckled and took a sip of his beer.

"Guess you're right, boy," he said. "Wouldn't do for the First Brother-in-law to parade around the streets in his BVDs, would it?"

"No, sir," the man said. He wasn't smiling. They never smiled. That's what Bobby Jack hated most

6

about the Secret Service. They never smiled. And they wouldn't have a beer with him, which was strange, because they didn't look like members of the international fag, liberal, Jewish conspiracy.

He sat on his bed with a sigh, pulled a pair of blue jeans from the floor and started to put them on.

What the hell had that reporter said about him and the National Jewish Alliance? Censured him? For what? He hadn't done a goddamn thing. He knew what it was. They were just trying to get at the president through him. If Bobby Jack had been president instead of being the president's brother-in-law, he would do something about the National Jewish Alliance and that *New York Times* and that guy on the editorial page who had it in for Bobby Jack. He wouldn't take it lying down. That's why he knew he'd never be any good in politics. He wasn't about to kiss anyone's ass just because they controlled banks and radio and television and newspapers and half the United States Senate. Someday he'd tell them that. Tell them just what he thought.

He got his jeans on but couldn't find a belt, but it didn't matter, he decided, because he wasn't into belts. They kind of constricted the free flow of his belly. He put on loafers without socks. He didn't need a shirt; his tee shirt was good for another day at least.

He stopped by the kitchen on his way out. He dropped his empty beer can into the open metal garbage can. The flies quickly rose to make room for it, then dropped to investigate. He took another can from the refrigerator, then grabbed a second

7

can and put it into his back pocket. You never could tell when you might run out.

The reporters were still waiting for him. The Secret Service men seemed to want to get Bobby Jack into a car and drive off, but Bobby Jack wanted to talk to the reporters. He could handle them. He had, back when his brother-in-law was running for president. The reporters had treated him as a charming rustic then. He hadn't changed a bit, so why should they change the way they wrote about him?

The reporters wanted to talk about the National Jewish Alliance.

"What is this here censure?" Bobby Jack asked one of them, a lean brunette with a big chest. "I thought censure was when you cut the good parts out of movies." He winked at her and sipped at his beer. He felt the two Secret Service men standing at his side on the dusty path. The reporters stood in front of him.

"The NJA said that you're a disgrace to America with your racist attitudes. They called you a vicious anti-Semite and asked the president to disavow your remarks. What's your reaction to that?"

"Well," Bobby Jack drawled casually, "Jews are always complaining about something. Why don't we forget that shit? I ever tell you the joke about the two niggers at the United Nations?"

He waited for an answer. That joke never failed. In the campaign, it had always been good for a chuckle from the newspapermen and they never wrote stories about it either. These reporters didn't seem to want to hear it.

Billings tossed his empty beer can out toward the

unpaved street. His bladder hurt. He should have gone to the bathroom again.

A neighbor passed and waved at him.

"Hiya, Bobby Jack."

" 'Lo, Luke. How's it hanging?"

"Straight, Bobby Jack."

"Keep it that way, Luke."

He smiled as the other man walked away. He realized though that his bladder was so full that even smiling hurt.

"Wait here a minute," he told the reporters.

A Secret Service man turned to walk with him.

"You stay here," Bobby Jack said. "Nobody goes with me when I pee."

Rather than go all the way inside, he walked alongside his house. He urinated against the wall of the building. He was zipping up his fly as he walked back to the reporters. The thin brunette looked as if she had just swallowed a lemon, peel and all.

Her tough luck, thought Bobby Jack. Did she think that men didn't have to pee once in a while? Maybe the men she went out with didn't.

He took the can of beer from his back pocket and snapped it open. The bouncing it had undergone caused the beer to spray up in the air. Quickly, he put his thumb over the hole and aimed the spray at the reporters. He caught the big-chested woman with a frothy spray that landed atop her curly sprayed hairdo, where it settled like droplets of dew on a spider web.

She slapped at her hair with her hand. Her face was contorted with annoyance.

"Jerk," she said.

9

"Liberal," Bobby Jack said.

"Asshole," she said.

"Jew," he said.

"Cretin," she said.

"Nigger lover," he said.

She turned and walked away from him. He looked after her appreciatively, then turned to the other two reporters who still stood there, wiping beer from their faces.

"Nice ass," Bobby Jack said, gesturing toward the woman. "You getting any of that?"

The two reporters looked at each other, then walked away, following the brunette.

Bobby Jack watched them go, then turned to the Secret Service men.

"Glad those creeps are gone," he said. "Got things to do."

There were no reporters at the dusty dry train station when Bobby Jack and the two Secret Service men arrived there in his black Chevrolet station wagon. The car annoyed Bobby Jack. Everybody in Washington had Cadillacs. Why did he have to settle for a black Chevrolet station wagon? He had mentioned it to his brother-in-law, who had told him what kind of car to buy, and had demanded an answer.

"Image," the president had said. "An image of economy."

"How come every time I want something you talk about economy?" Bobby Jack had demanded. "I never hear economy about niggers."

"Stop using that word," the president said.

10

"All right. Coloreds," Bobby Jack replied. "Why just me for economy?"

"Because you don't know how to act," the president told him. "The last thing you wanted was Air Force One to use to go duck hunting on weekends. They'd fry me for that. Then you wanted the presidential helicopter to go into the woods for a nudist beer bash with your buddies. I'm not God. I'm just the president."

"Yeah, 'cause I helped make you the president and you don't seem to remember that most of the time, and it's a helluva way to treat kin."

"By marriage," the president had said.

Bobby Jack sat on the edge of the back train platform and looked at his watch. It was 10 A.M. He finished his last can of beer and decided he would give these goddamn Arabs exactly five minutes before he left to get a refill.

He didn't need Arabs and he didn't like the way they looked or talked or dressed or smelled. And he didn't need their money. He had money of his own. He had the old shoe factory where business was never better and he had a lot of other money besides.

At 10:04 A.M., just as he was rising to his feet, he heard the rumble of a train far down the track. He looked toward the north and saw the engine, pulling a single car, come over the slight rise and down the long incline that led into the bucolic town of Hills, its brakes squeaking and hissing air as it slowed down. Inside the building that doubled as passenger terminal and control center, an engineer pressed an automatic switch that turned a section

11

of track so it would deflect the train off onto a siding. The train pulled into the siding and shivered to a halt.

Bobby Jack continued to sit on the train platform. After a few minutes, three men in Arab robes stepped out onto the rear of the railroad car, saw him, and came down the steps.

They carefully crossed the double sets of tracks and came up to him.

"I am Mustafa Kaffir," one man said. He was a big man with dark skin and the nose of an eagle. "And these are—"

"Don't bother," Bobby Jack said. He remained sitting. "I'm awful with names and besides all Ayrab names sound alike."

Kaffir coughed slightly and said, "They too are representatives of the Free People's Government of Libya."

"Sure, swell," said Bobby Jack.

"Where may we talk?" Kaffir asked. His deepset eyes glanced left and right. His thin lips were closed tightly as if he found the small Southern village of Hills somehow distasteful.

"Right here's fine by me," Bobby Jack said. He followed Kaffir's eyes as they glanced toward the two Secret Service men who leaned against the wall of the railroad station.

"Hey," Billings called. "You two get lost a while. I got to talk a spell here with my good Ay-rab friends."

"We'll be in front," the taller agent said.

"Yeah, good. Wait out in front. When I'm done here, we'll go get a drink somewhere."

His eyes followed them as they left, then he

glanced back at Kaffir. The Libyan was sweating, even though it was only in the low 90s, a relatively cool summer day in Hills. Funny, he hadn't thought Arabs sweated. If they sweated in America, they must really sweat in Arabia or wherever the hell they came from. That must be some place to smell.

"All right," Bobby Jack said. "They're gone. What's on your mind?"

"You know what we seek?" Kaffir said. The two men stood behind him. They seemed to be trying to hunch up their shoulders to keep the bottoms of their long flowing robes out of the dust of the train platform.

"I think so, but suppose you tell me," Bobby Jack said.

"The Free People's Government of Libya wishes to purchase plutonium from your government."

"What do you want me for?"

"Because your government's policy is to refuse to sell plutonium to Libya. We thought perhaps your influence could change that policy, particularly since we want it to build only peaceful nuclear power plants that will enable us to increase the standard of living for millions of people in the Arab world. It is only a lie that we would attempt to make nuclear weapons to attack Israel. We would never attack Israel. We would only defend ourselves."

Billings nodded. "Wouldn't hurt my feelings if you did attack them."

"No?" said Kaffir.

"Not at all. And when you wipe them out in Tel Aviv, I wish you'd get rid of them in New York."

Mustafa Kaffir smiled gently and sadly, as if he

13

had often dreamed such dreams. The two men behind him nodded vigorously.

"Well, that is a matter for others," said Kaffir. "I,
sir, am here only to purchase plutonium for peaceful purposes."

"And you want me to talk to my brother-in-law
to get him to allow that sale," Bobby Jack said.

"That is correct, because we know you have
much influence with the president."

"Right," said Billings. "Me and my sister. Only
people he listens to." He paused. "And what do I
get out of it?"

"In such international arrangements, a finder's fee
is often paid the one who makes it all possible,"
Kaffir said.

"How much?"

"This fee is a perfectly legitimate item," Kaffir
said.

"How much?"

"Of course, it would have to be—"

"How much!" Billings insisted.

"One million dollars," Kaffir said.

"All right," said Bobby Jack. "Two hundred thou
down."

"I beg your pardon."

"Two hundred thousand down. In advance. Non-
refundable. Whether I succeed or not. I've got to
have something to reimburse me for my time, even
if I can't get the okay."

Kaffir thought for a moment, his dark eyes scru-
tinizing the open face of Bobby Jack Billings.

Billings stood up from his seat on the platform
edge.

14

"You talk it over with the other Ay-rabs," he said. "I gotta go tap a kidney."

He walked away from the three Libyans toward the far end of the platform. They'd go for it, he knew. It was only two hundred thousand dollars, tax-free and unrecorded. He had made exactly the same deal four other times before. He had promised the Rhodesian Communists that he would make sure of their recognition by the U.S. He had promised a Red Chinese delegation that America would hand over Taiwan. He had promised Iranian rebels that he could prevent the United States from stepping in to keep the shah in power. The only thing he had failed on was a promise to get the president to send in troops to help bail out Idi Amin's imperiled regime in Uganda.

But three out of four wasn't bad for no work, he thought. His practice on all such contracts was the same. He took the money and then forgot about the contract. Most of the time it turned out all right, because his brother-in-law's foreign policy often seemed to have been drawn up in the back seat of Fidel Castro's car.

Of course, the people he dealt with never knew that, and probably would not have believed it even if Bobby Jack had told them. They were sure the only reason they had succeeded was because they had a friend at the highest level—Bobby Jack—whispering in the president's ear.

As he reached the corner of the platform, Billings looked back to see the three Libyans staring at him. He unzipped his fly and pointed at his groin.

15

"Just got to make a little tinkle against the wall here," he said. "Be right back."

Mustafa Kaffir nodded. When Billings jumped down from the platform to the dirt alongside the building, Kaffir broke into animated conversation with his two companions, speaking Arabic.

They had all decided to go for the deal. After all, two hundred thousand dollars was a small down payment for the ingredients necessary to build atomic bombs to destroy Israel. But they agreed to seem reluctant to pay such a large amount. If they looked too willing, Billings might ask for more. But they knew the price was right. After all, hadn't Billings managed to make the president withhold American recognition of a free government in Rhodesia, instead throwing its lot in with Communist-backed rebels? Had Billings not convinced the president to disregard the treaties America had with Taiwan? Had Billings not kept the president immobile when America's staunchest friend in the Middle East, the shah of Iran, was being overthrown by an American-hating rebel band? The man might be a sweat-smelling ignorant clod, Mustafa Kaffir thought, but he knew how to move the American government. His record of success was untouched. At two hundred thousand dollars down payment, he was a bargain.

Kaffir and his two companions waited for Bobby Jack to return. After five minutes, one of the men wanted to look for him.

"He was going to urinate. He should be back by now," the man said. He was the Libyan minister of finance.

"Not yet," the other man said. He was the minister of culture. "Maybe he had to make number two."

The finance minister giggled.

"Silence," said Kaffir in Arabic.

They waited ten more minutes.

"Perhaps he has forgotten," said the minister of culture.

"Who forgets two hundred thousand dollars who wears such clothes and urinates against walls?" asked Kaffir. "Wait here."

He walked to the far end of the platform. He stopped just before the corner of the building.

"Mr. Billings. Are you there?"

There was no answer and Mustafa Kaffir leaned around the corner and looked along the red-painted wooden wall of the old frame building.

Bobby Jack Billings was not there.

There was a wet stain in the sandy soil showing where he had stood a few minutes before, but the man himself was gone. Mustafa Kaffir looked around. He saw railroad tracks, open fields, and occasional houses several hundred yards away, but no sign of Bobby Jack Billings.

Kaffir signaled his two men to follow him and they walked together to the front of the railroad station. The only persons in sight were the two Secret Service agents sitting inside a black Chevrolet station wagon with the air conditioner running.

As the three Libyans approached them, the agents stepped out of the car.

"Yes, sir," said the older one.

"Where is Mr. Billings?"

The agent looked startled.

"I left him with you," he said.

17

"Yes. But he walked away and did not come back," Kaffir said.

"Oh, shit," the agent said.

The second agent had opened the car door and was reaching for a radio phone. "Should I call in?" he asked.

"Not yet," the first agent said. "Let's take a look around. Maybe he just went to take a piss or steal a beer somewhere."

Mustafa Kaffir showed the agents where Bobby Jack Billings had stood to urinate against the wall of the station building.

The tall agent knelt down to look closer at the ground. The dusty soil was packed hard where Bobby Jack's feet would have been. The agent stuck a finger into the dirt and felt metal. He brushed dirt away.

He found two pieces of metal: a small golden Star of David and a small iron swastika.

"What the hell does that mean?" he said aloud to himself. He lifted the two pieces of metal in a handkerchief and dropped them into his pocket.

He looked up as the second Secret Service man approached, shaking his head.

"They just took me all over the train," the agent said. "He's not in there."

"Shit," said the older agent. "Better call in for help."

"You know he's gonna turn up in some saloon, don't you?"

"Sure I do, but we've gotta call in anyway. You make sure those Arabs wait here and I'll call headquarters."

The radio phone was answered immediately in

18

the Secret Service field office in Atlanta, Georgia.

"This is Gavone," the older agent said with the dry, bored, laconic voice usually affected by airline pilots whose planes were plunging nose-first into an ocean. "Got a little problem."

"What's that?" responded another dry voice.

"We think the Link is missing."

"Look under a porch someplace. He's probably sleeping one off."

"We looked," Gavone said. "He's gone. Better send help."

"You're serious, aren't you?"

"Deadly serious. Hurry up, will you?"

"Shit," said the voice in Atlanta. "The Missing Link. Just what we need."

CHAPTER TWO

His name was Remo and he was going to do something about pollution in America.

He stood on a hill looking down at three tall smokestacks that jutted up into the sky, puffing out wisps of thin white smoke. It was coal smoke, Remo knew, but it had been washed and filtered and processed until it was cleaner than the smoke from oil furnaces. The cleansing process had raised the price of using coal until it was higher than that of using oil bought from the Arabs. But it was all America had—high-priced oil or equally high-priced coal. Nuclear power was dead in the water. A small accident in which not one person was injured—no person had ever been injured in a nuclear accident in America—had been turned into the scare story of the century by the media, and by the time it was over, the drive toward nuclear power was scuttled. Remo thought it was sad that the country that had developed and pioneered nuclear power someday probably would be the only country in the industrial world not to use it. The marchers had won again.

They were the same marchers who had welcomed the Vietcong victory in Vietnam and so weakened America's will that the United States pulled out of the Far East and let it be overrun by the communists. A long night of terror had descended over that part of the world. In Cambodia the illiteracy rate had reached 99 percent because everybody who could read or write had been murdered. It was a country with six doctors for six million people. Somehow, the marchers had nothing to say about that.

Remo had decided a long time before that America had lost more than face when it quit the war in Vietnam. It had lost America; it had lost its spirit. Formosa was given up, Iran was lost. In southern Africa, America had made it clear that the only government it would recognize would be a government made up of Communist terrorists—no matter how the people of that region voted. A college professor whose primary qualification was that she hated America had gone to Russia to receive an award from the Communists and said that all the talk about Soviet persecution of dissidents was a smokescreen to cover up America's persecution of dissidents. And then she had gone back to her publicly paid position on the faculty of a state-supported college.

So much pollution, Remo thought, as he looked down into the small valley at the five thousand people who were camped outside the fences of the small coal-burning electrical generation plant. He turned to the small Oriental next to him and said sadly, "Chiun, it's all over."

"What is?" the Oriental said. He was only five

feet tall, almost a foot shorter than Remo. He continued to look down at the crowd, the thin wisps of white beard and hair around his ears puffing occasionally in a stray breeze.

"America," Remo said. "We're done."

"Does this mean we are finally leaving to find work elsewhere?" Chium asked. He looked toward Remo who was still staring down at the crowd. "I have told you many times there is no shortage of countries that would be glad to have two premier assassins performing for them." Chiun's voice was high-pitched but strong, a voice that seemed too strong to come from a man who appeared to be eighty years old and frail. The old Oriental wore a bright white brocade kimono and despite the summer heat of Pennsylvania, he did not sweat.

"No," Remo said. "It does not mean that we are going to look for work elsewhere. It's just kind of sad that no matter what we do, America is shot."

"I have never understood this," Chium said. "You act as if America were something special, but it is not special. It is just another country. Think of the grandeur that was Greece, the glory that was Rome, gone in the mists of time. All that is left is men who dance with each other and women who cook spaghetti. Think of the pharaohs and their empires. Think of the blond Macedonian. All gone. Should America be different?"

"Yes," Remo said stubbornly.

"You can explain why?"

"Because this country is free. All those other places you mentioned, there was no freedom. But here people are free. And we're being conquered from inside. We're being torn up by Americans."

"That is the way it is with freedom," Chium said. "Give people freedom and many of them will use it to fight you."

"So what's the answer?" Remo asked. "Take away freedom?"

The wizened old man looked up at the sky before replying. A lone chicken hawk patrolled the bright white skies. "The House of Sinanju has been in many nations for many centuries," he said.

"I know," said Remo. "Please, no history lectures."

"All I wish to say was that this was the first country I had ever learned of which seemed to be run by caprice and whimsy. It is as if the tiniest minority runs this nation, and it is always that minority which hates the country most."

"I know that," Remo said. "So remove the freedom? That's the answer?

"No," Chiun said. "Remove the freedom and you will be conquered from outside. Keep the freedom and you will be destroyed from inside."

"So there's no hope," Remo said.

"None at all," Chiun said. "All nations die. The only thing wrong with your nation's death is that it will be inglorious. Better to die before the sword than before the germ." He looked down again at the five thousand people lounging around before the electric company gates, a few of them shouting slogans and singing. "Take heart with one thing, though," he said.

"What's that?" Remo asked.

"Those germs down there. When this country gives way to whatever will follow it, be assured that they will be the first to go."

Remo shook his head. "It all makes you feel hopeless."

"No, no," Chiun said quickly. "We have our art. The fullness of our lives comes from within. It requires nothing else."

"Except targets," Remo said.

"That is true," Chiun said. "I stand corrected. Assassins need targets."

Suddenly Remo was angry and he waved his hand at the marchers milling around below and said, "There should be enough targets there to satisfy anyone."

"I will wait for you here," Chiun said. "Enjoy yourself. But restrain your anger."

"I will," Remo said as he moved quickly down the hill. This was the fifth day the electric plant had been shut down by the pickets who surrounded it. The demonstrators had also made a daily run at the fence surrounding the plant and each day had been held off by the beleaguered town and plant police. But this day was different, Remo had heard. He had gotten word from upstairs that guns and explosives had been shipped in to the demonstrators.

With the plant closed down, one hundred thousand families had been without electricity for five days. No refrigeration, no electric lights, no television and no radio. Hospitals were using emergency generators to perform major surgery and if any of those generators failed, people would die because there were no more backup systems.

The crowd around the electric plant was like a small declivity in marshland. When the tide came in, it filled, and when the tide went out, it emptied.

Except that the television cameras were the water pressure that filled and emptied this pool of people. When the TV cameras were on, they charged the fence and surged and chanted, and when the cameramen had gone, the pickets pulled back away from the fence, leaving behind a landscape littered with broken frisbees, sandwich wrappers, plastic Big Mac containers, the stubs of hand-rolled cigarettes, and the remnants of their signs opposing dirty air and "the polluting coal interests."

This was a low tide time. Remo moved through the large crowd, which hung out in lethargic groups, many of them lying on their backs working on their suntans. Others shared beer. Vendors were selling sunflower seeds. A hundred feet away, a half-dozen uniformed policemen guarded the plant gates, but even they stood relaxed, knowing that the absence of TV cameras had lulled everything into a kind of truce.

Remo did not expect to find the person he was looking for. No one looked at him as he walked around through the small clusters of people.

"Hey, man, got a smoke?" somebody asked him.

"No," Remo said.

"Come on, gimme a smoke," the man said. He grabbed Remo's shoulder. Remo turned to look at him. He was a thin man in his mid-forties wearing a powder-blue polyester leisure suit and white patent leather shoes. Remo wondered what he was doing there. Weren't revolutionaries supposed to stop revolting when they got older? They weren't supposed to switch from jeans to leisure suits and keep doing the same old thing in different clothes.

"Aren't you a little old for this?" Remo asked. He

27

disengaged the man's hand from his shoulder. The man felt his hand go numb. But it did not hurt; that would come later.

"Yeah, I suppose so, but what the hell, this is where the chickies are."

Remo shrugged.

"But you need grass to score," the man said. "You really do. Come on. I gotta make some grass."

"I'd like to see you all making grass," Remo said. "From underneath."

"Owwww, my hand hurts. What'd you do to it?"

"Enjoy it," Remo said. "It's organic pain. The real thing."

"You're not funny," the man said. He wore a vasectomy pin in his lapel. "What are you doing here anyway?"

"I'm looking for Janie Baby," Remo said. She was an internationally known folk singer who had made a fortune in America, then moved to London where she unleashed a continuing series of broadsides at racist, imperialist, war-mongering America. She had stayed in London five years, until the British had raised their tax rate into the ninety percent range, whereupon she had moved back to America and married an attorney who had gained notoriety by defending protest leaders in the Sixties. He was called the intellectual force behind the protest movement, which was not all that difficult, considering that most of the protesters regarded logic as a middle-class white American trick to enslave the blacks and the poor.

"She said she's coming back later. She's probably in her room in town," the man said. He tried to rub

28

his hand, but when he touched it, it hurt and he made a grimace of pain.

"Thanks," Remo said. "Watch out for that hand." In her room in town? Remo doubted it. The shutdown of electricity would have shut down the air conditioning in her suite and in the extreme summer heat, she was not going to be in any uncooled room if she didn't have to be.

Remo trotted back up the hill and collected Chiun who seemingly had not moved a muscle since Remo had left. They drove back into the small town of Clairburg and Remo stopped alongside a policeman doing traffic duty.

"Officer," he called.

The policeman flinched as if expected to be attacked. His hand crept toward his holster. Then he saw Remo and relaxed at the sight of an adult.

"Yes," he said.

"With all the power off," Remo said, "where's the nearest motel with air conditioning?"

"Let's see," the cop said. He thought for a moment. Remo could see the man's lips moving. "The nearest one'd be the Makeshift Motel, four miles outside town. On Route 90. Go straight, this turns right into it. You a reporter?"

"No," Remo said.

"Good. I hate reporters."

"Don't weaken and don't falter," Remo said as he drove off.

The Makeshift Motel was only five minutes away, spread out alongside the road like four ranch homes that had decided to go through life together. Remo parked in the oversized lot, and Chiun waited in the car while the younger man went into the office.

There was a blonde young woman in the office, flanked by two plastic ferns. She wore a pink sweater and white slacks and she smiled warmly when her eyes met Remo's eyes, which were so dark that they might be black. Remo was almost six feet tall and slim, with thick wrists that protruded from his rolled-up shirt sleeves.

"Where is she?" Remo said.

"Where's who?"

"C'mon, I don't have a lot of time. My crew's waiting outside and we've got to hurry to get this on the seven o'clock network news. Where is she?"

He drummed his fingers on the countertop.

"I'll take you to her," the girl said.

Remo shook his head.

"No. Just let me get this interview done and then I'll have some time to come back to talk to you."

"Promise?"

"Cross my heart and hope to die," Remo said.

"Room 27. End of the wing," the girl said, pointing toward a window.

"Anybody in the rooms around them?" Remo asked.

The girl threw Remo a nervous little glance. He explained quickly, "Nothing ruins an interview faster than somebody talking in the next room. You'll find that out when you're on television yourself."

The girl nodded. "No. Nobody on either side. They wanted it that way."

"Thanks. I'll be back."

30

Back at the car, Remo told Chiun, "I'll be a few minutes."

"Take your time. Just don't be untidy."

Remo heard voices inside Room 27 and went back to Room 26. The door was locked but he vibrated the knob quickly in his hand, back and forth, until the metal parts slipped and the knob turned easily. He locked the door quickly behind him.

Listening at the connecting doors between the rooms, Remo heard and recognized two of the voices.

There was Janie Baby, with her well-bred nasal whine that somehow changed into a smooth liquid soprano when she began to sing. There was the languid voice of her consort, the revolutionary lawyer-theoretician who lived with her in Malibu. Remo did not recognize any of the other voices.

Janie Baby: "Tony, run over the plan one more time so we all know what we're doing."

Tony: "I've gone over it three times already."

Janie Baby: "Then this time should be easy for you. Once more."

Cheer up, Remo thought. That's the price you have to pay for being the royal stud. It could have been worse. One of the other well-known protest leaders was wanted for selling drugs; another had married a Hollywood star and joined the middle class; another one was shilling for a guru.

Tony: "We bring the guns in under the boxes of food and hand them out. Janie, at 8:30, you call the press to a meeting at the rear of the crowd. That way, they won't be able to see anything. When you get started, we'll get the crowd to surge toward the

31

gates. Our people will fire a couple of shots. The cops will fire back. By the time the press gets back there, it'll be a full-scale riot. Of course, we'll have witnesses who say the cops fired first. When the mob pushes through the gate, we'll have the explosives stashed next to the generator station in a box that looks like a reel of electric cable. We'll be long gone 'cause there's no point in taking a chance on getting hurt. Then after they put down the riot, probably during the night we'll trigger the explosives by radio and blow up the whole frigging plant."

Unknown voice: "People might get hurt."

Janie Baby: "You can't make an omelet without breaking some eggs."

Tony: "Right. That's not our problem. Anyway, tomorrow Janie'll hold a press conference and blame the shooting on the cops. We'll phony up some witnesses who saw them fire first."

Unknown voice: "What about the explosion?"

Janie Baby: "Leave that to me. It just proves what a shoddy unsafe operation this coal-burning monster is. Where's the radio transmitter to set off the charge?"

Tony: "It's under my mattress. We'll leave it there until we want it. So there's no accident."

Unknown voice: "I've put the guns at the bottom of the box of chicken salad sandwiches. It's marked on top."

Janie Baby: "Good. And the explosives?"

Voice: "Already in the trunk of the car."

Pause.

Janie Baby: "Okay. It's almost seven o'clock. We better get moving."

Remo waited while people shuffled around in the next room, then heard the front door open and close. He glanced out the edge of the drape at the front window and saw the singer, her husband and two other men walking toward a white Lincoln sedan, dripping with chrome and doodads. Presumably, Remo thought, their grass-fueled Volkswagen was at the florist for repairs.

There was no knob on Remo's side of the connecting doors, just a round smooth lock plate. Remo brought his right hand back to his hip and punched with his hard fingertips into the wood next to the round brass plate. The wood splintered as Remo's fingers drove into the core of the door. His fingertips nicked the lock mechanism, turned it and the door pushed open.

The single room looked like an illegal dump. Neither bed was made. A wastepaper basket was filled with beer cans and wine bottles and when it had overflowed, the room's occupants had made do by throwing cans and bottles anywhere. Butcher paper from sandwiches littered the floor. Half-eaten heroes were dropped on the dresser.

Remo peeked into the bathroom, curious to see how the well-bred who wanted to bring America to a new and brighter tomorrow of freedom and personal responsibility lived. The sink was pocked with beard stubble, but the free motel soap had not been opened. The bath towels had not been touched and the shower and tub were dry and unused. There were four beer cans on the vanity shelf next to the sink. There was a half-empty jar of no-fluorocarbon anti-perspirant next to the sink, along

33

with a dozen cylindrical plastic bottles of multi-colored pills.

"Better living through chemistry," Remo said aloud. He went back into the main room and flipped the mattress from one bed onto the floor. There was no radio transmitter under it.

Remo lifted up the second mattress and saw the transmitter, a square black box with dials, a chrome button and a pull-up antenna. Behind him, he heard the front door open.

"Well, well, well, what have we here?" a voice asked.

Remo looked over his shoulder and said, "Maid service. This room was due for a cleaning in 1946 and somehow we missed it."

The man standing in the doorway was a large blond with a slick brown tan. He wore white jeans. His biceps bulged from under his short-sleeved tan shirt and his lat muscles rippled as he folded his arms and looked at the radio transmitter on the bed.

"What's that?" he asked.

"A new organic mini-vacuum cleaner," Remo said. "It gets rid of all kinds of dirt. Want to see how it works?"

"No, wiseass. I just want to see you in the slammer for burglary."

He came into the room and closed the door behind him. Remo picked up the radio transmitter and let the mattress collapse back onto the bed. The blond man reached for the telephone on the end table near the door.

"Can't let you do that, friend," Remo said.

"Try and stop me," the burly blond said.

34

"Whatever makes you happy," Remo said.

He walked casually toward the blond who now had the phone in his hand. Remo reached out a finger and depressed the cutoff button.

The blond, with a nasty sneer on his face, tried to do two things at once. He slammed the receiver back down, hoping to smash it onto Remo's finger, and with the heel of his left hand he pushed at Remo's chest to try to shove him back into the room.

The receiver hit the phone base but missed Remo's finger. The blond felt his right hand being removed from the instrument by Remo's left hand. The heel of the big man's left hand slammed squarely against Remo's chest. To the blond, it felt like butting his hand against a brick wall. The shock wave raced back through his wrist, up his forearm and upper arm and made his shoulder shudder.

He swung wildly at Remo's head with his right hand. The punch missed.

"Isn't there any way you're going to behave yourself?" Remo asked.

"I'm gonna take your head off, sucker," the blond said.

Remo sighed. The blond threw another left hand and right hand at the slim man standing in front of him. Remo did not move, but somehow both punches missed. It was as if the smaller man had kept his feet rooted but had just swayed left and right out of the reach of the punches. The blond felt his long back muscles stretching painfully when the punches missed. He grabbed at the telephone and slapped it towards Remo's temple, but the instrument went over the top of Remo's head as he ducked. Then, as Remo came up, the blond felt himself lifted high into the air, and his 240 pounds were being thrown toward the back of the motel room. He wasn't spry enough or quick-witted enough to cushion his head before he butted skull first into the wall. The crunch of his head hitting the wall punched a foot-wide soft spot into the sheetrock of the wall, beneath the cheap metallic vinyl wallcovering. The blond groaned and fell into a lump.

Remo walked out the front door without looking back. If the man wasn't dead, that was all right. And if he was dead, that was all right too. What mattered was the big ugly Lincoln and making sure it did not get too far away.

He put the radio transmitter on the seat between himself and Chuin as he got into the rented car and drove quickly from the motel parking lot.

When he reached Clairburg four miles away, he saw the white Lincoln four cars ahead of him. With luck, he would get close on the open stretch of highway leading from the town to the electrical station.

They were just passing out of the town and moving back onto the main highway when Chuin said, "You are not going to tell me, are you?"

"Tell you what?"

"What is this black box?"

Remo watched ahead. The other cars had moved away from between his car and the white Lincoln. There was only three hundred yards now between the cars and Remo was steadily closing the gap.

"It's a toy," Remo said.

"How does it work?" Chuin asked. His long-

36

fingernailed hands moved over to pick up the black box.

"I'll explain," Remo said. "First pull up the antenna."

Chiun's long fingers nipped at the round ball at the top of the retractible antenna and pulled it up to its full 15-inch height.

"What now?" he asked.

"There's a switch there that says on-off. Turn it to on," Remo said.

Without looking, he heard Chiun click the switch. He was only a hundred yards now behind the Lincoln. There were no other cars visible on the road.

"What next?" Chiun said. "Must I always drag everything out of you?"

"There is a battery/indicator light next to the on-off switch," Remo said. "Tell me when it comes on."

"I like this," Chiun said. "I really like this."

"Just watch for the light," Remo said.

"It's on," Chiun said. "It's on. An orange light. It just came on."

Seventy-five yards.

"Now you see that button on top?" Remo asked.

"Yes."

"Do you know what'll happen if you press it?"

"What?" asked Chiun.

Fifty yards.

"Try it and find out."

"I want to know first," Chiun said. "What will happen if I press it?" But even as he spoke his index finger reached toward the chrome button.

"Watch that car up there," Remo said. Chiun looked up as he pressed the button.

37

There was a muffled thump in the Lincoln ahead of them and then a large explosion that lifted the car six feet up into the air. Sheets of white metal ripped from the car while it was airborne and flew even higher into the air. While the car was still off the ground, the gas tank exploded and turned the car into an oblong ball of flame, which hit back onto the roadway and careened forward until it slammed against a metal and concrete retaining wall.

It burned. There would be no gunfights tonight at the electrical station. No bombs planted. No semi-innocent people killed. Remo felt good about it.

Without slowing down, he skidded a U-turn in the highway, jumped the low concrete center divider and drove back toward the town.

"A boom," Chiun said.

"Bomb," said Remo. "And remember, no complaints about bombs ruining the perfection of an assassination. You did it yourself."

"You mean every time I press this button, a car will blow up?"

"No," said Remo.

"It has to be a white car?"

"No."

"An ugly white car?"

"No," said Remo. "It'll never work again."

Chiun rolled down his window and tossed the black transmitter far out into the weeds lining the road.

"Junk," he said. "What good is a piece of junk that only works once?"

"Just what I was thinking," Remo said.

* * *

There was a message for them when they returned to their motel room. Remo was to call his Aunt Lorraine right away. That meant Harold W. Smith, director of the secret agency CURE for which Remo worked as an assassin. This week it was Aunt Lorraine. Last week, it had been Uncle Howard and the week before that, Cousin Doreen. Remo wondered if the republic's secrets would really all go down the tube if the CURE director simply left a message for Remo to call Smith.

When the clerk told him that he should call Aunt Lorraine, Remo decided to test his theory.

"I don't have an Aunt Lorraine," he said.

"But that's what the message was," the clerk said. "Really. I took the call myself."

"Yes, but that's just a code," Remo said. "That's from a man named Smith who wants me to call him."

There was a pause. The clerk said, "Then why didn't he just say to call Mr. Smith?"

"Because he's afraid you'll tell the Russians. Worse yet, the Congress."

"Oh, I see," the clerk said. "Well, I have other things to do, sir, so I'd better get off this line."

"You're not calling the Russians, are you?" Remo asked.

"No, sir."

"All right. You'd better not because Smitty gets upset about things like that," Remo said.

The clerk gave him an open line and Remo dialed an 800 area code number which went through two switching devices before it finally rang inside a sanitarium in Rye, New York, where

CURE's headquarters maintained its cover operation.

"Remo here," said Remo.

Smith's dry voice started out without any identification, but there was no mistaking the acid tones.

"Remo, do you know who Bobby Jack Billings is?"

Remo thought a moment before a picture of a fat face with a beer can implanted came into his mind.

"Yeah. He's the president's uncle or something."

"Brother-in-law," Smith said. "He's been kidnapped."

"Sounds good to me," Remo said as he hung up the telephone and disconnected it from the wall.

CHAPTER THREE

"This is one fine dumb place to meet," Remo said.

"Think of that the next time you're disconnecting your telephone," Smith said.

It was 2 A.M. Remo had just stepped into the New York City subway car at 56th Street and Sixth Avenue. Dr. Harold W. Smith, wearing a gray suit and carrying a briefcase, already sat on one of the molded fiberglass seats. The rest of the car was empty, but bore unmistakable evidence of having been infested by Homo New Yorkis in the recent past. Vile graffiti were spray-painted on the walls. Obscene suggestions were Magic-Markered onto the metal panels. Most of the subway advertising signs had been ripped down but the few that remained had been turned into hand-drawn displays of immense genitalia. The car reeked of the residual acrid smell of marijuana smoke.

Remo looked around in disgust. He remembered a book he had seen a few years before in which the author had tried to justify these depredations by calling them a new kind of urban folk art. Remo had discounted it then because the author was a violence junkie whose weakness was finding truth, beauty and the eternal verities in prizefighting, war, riots, rape and robbery.

"We could have met in a restaurant," Remo said as he slid next to Smith on the seat. "It didn't have to be here."

"Congress is acting up again. We can't be too careful," Smith said.

"The chain still stops at the president," Remo said. "Nobody gets to us until he cracks."

"That's true,' Smith said noncommittally. His voice was dry and pinched as if expressiveness cost money and he was not inclined to waste any.

The train lurched around a tunnel corner, its metal wheels screaming at an intense pitch that Remo found painful to his ears.

"At any rate," Smith said, "it appears that Bobby Jack Billings has been kidnapped."

"Who'd want him?" Remo said.

"I don't know. There has been no ransom demand."

"He's probably off on a bat somewhere," Remo said.

Smith shook his head. He adjusted his briefcase on his lap as if points might be taken off his final mark in life for lack of neatness. "He's too well known," he said. "He would have been spotted somewhere, but instead he has vanished." Smith quickly sketched the facts of Bobby Jack Billings's disappearance.

As the car rolled to a stop at 51st Street, Remo shook his head.

"A Star of David *and* a swastika at the scene?"

"Correct," Smith said. "Of course we checked it

43

but it was just costume junk jewelry and could have been purchased anywhere."

"And the last people who saw him were Arabs?" Remo asked.

"Libyans," Smith said. "Yes."

"I don't know what you think but I think it's all a crock."

"You find it a little unbelievable?" Smith said.

"A lot unbelievable."

"So do I."

Smith lurched back in his seat as the train jerked away from the platform where it had stopped. "However," he said, "it's possible that some group with overseas ties kidnapped Billings. The president is inordinately fond of him, and might be blackmailed into doing something or other. That's not the possibility that worries me, though."

"What is?"

"That the president ordered the kidnapping himself," Smith said.

Remo shook his head. "I can't see that," he said. "Remember, you're talking about Washington. The president and his whole staff would be lucky to find a restaurant that serves eggs. They couldn't pull off a kidnapping. And even if they did, what for?"

"Perhaps to put Billings on ice until after the election campaign. He *is* a constant embarrassment to them."

"If they did that, why did the president ask us to look into it?" Remo asked.

"He didn't," Smith said. "We came onto it through our other sources." He sat quietly. He did not name the sources, nor did he need to. Remo

44

knew that CURE was hooked in by computer and telephone and informant to every law enforcement agency in the country. No money moved, no crimes were investigated, very little happened in the nation without its being fed through interlocking networks into the massive CURE memory banks in Rye, New York.

"I give up," Remo said. "What do you want me to do?"

"Check out the Secret Service agents who were assigned to protect Billings. It's just possible they know something. If not, perhaps the Libyans who were meeting with him that day. I have all their names here," Smith said. As he drew a paper from his briefcase, the train lurched to a noisy screaming stop. Remo took the paper, folded it and put it into his pocket.

The automatic door opened and three young men came onto the train, surrounded by din. One had a portable radio blaring disco at full volume. The second carried a paper bag and the third carried a portable ladder.

From the paper bag, one of the youths pulled a bottle of wine which they passed around and slurped noisily. The youth with the radio put it on a seat where it continued to blare. He wore a denim Eisenhower jacket with an embroidered dragon on the back. The other two opened up the metal stepladder in the middle of the aisle.

Remo watched them as he told Smith, "Okay, we'll check it out. Do the Libyans know he's gone?"

"They might have guessed," Smith said. "The day after the incident, they received apologies from the president who told them his brother-in-law had just had too much to drink and had wandered off to a friend's house and fallen asleep. Maybe they bought it; I don't know. Then the White House released a picture of Billings playing volleyball near his home. It was an old photo from their files, taken last summer, but no one knows that and it might have satisfied the Libyans that Bobby Jack's still around." He looked at the three youths. "Don't they have guards on these trains?"

"Sure," Remo said, "but they're all hiding in the front car with the conductor."

A voice from the front of the car roared out over the volume of the radio.

"I don't know that I like all these people riding on our train."

Remo looked up. The young man with the radio was glaring at him. Remo stuck his tongue out at him.

"Hey, what you doing, man?" the youth bellowed. He turned down the radio.

"Trying to show the total revulsion I feel when I look at you," Remo said.

"You hear that? You hear that?" the youth demanded of his two friends who were pulling cans of spray paint from the large paper bag. "He insult us, man. I think revulsion is an insult."

"Your life is an insult," Remo said. "Shut up and keep that radio turned off."

"Yeah?" the young man said. He turned the radio back up to full volume.

Smith said to Remo, "Please."

"Please, my ass," Remo said.

The man with the radio had risen to his feet and looked menacingly at Remo who also stood up. He was shorter and thinner than the man with the radio.

"See that," the youth demanded of his friends. "He challenges us. He wants to fight."

One of his companions was standing halfway up the ladder, spraying white paint over the ceiling of the subway car. The other youth stood at the bottom, steadying the ladder, and holding in his arms two more cans of spray paint. They were very well organized, Remo conceded. Apparently they were going to paint over some of the graffiti on the ceiling and then repaint it with messages of their own choosing. The two youths ignored their friend who kept shouting, "He want to fight, he want to fight."

"How come you can't talk right?" Remo asked. He walked toward the three, brushing past the youth who was steadying the ladder. He plucked the large radio from the subway seat, dropped it onto the floor of the car and drove the heel of his shoe into it. The radio died with a suffering growl.

The sudden silence in the car attracted the attention of the two young men at the ladder. They looked toward Remo who stood in front of the youth wearing the Eisenhower jacket. The youth on the ladder dropped his can of spray paint on the seat and hopped down to the floor.

Remo realized all three were drunk. He remembered a time long ago, before he had come to work for CURE. He had been a policeman in New Jersey, sent to an electric chair that didn't work for a crime he didn't commit, and then he had joined CURE as its assassination arm under the tutlage of Chiun, the Korean assassin. In those old days in New Jersey, Remo had gotten drunk many a night.

But when he had been drunk, he hadn't tried to beat up on people or shove his radio noise down their ears. He had been a pleasant drunk who minded his own business, didn't speak unless spoken to and smiled a lot. Whatever happened to happy drunks, Remo wondered.

Still, because he remembered the long ago, it saved the three young men's lives. They charged Remo. He backed up to the bench seat, where he grabbed the spray can of white paint. As they flailed their arms about, trying to punch him, Remo moved in and out among them, depressing the red plastic button atop the can, and spraying white paint over their faces.

The train careened to an all-brake stop at Fourteenth Street. The doors opened and, one by one, Remo threw the three young men out onto the platform, easily dodging their wild swings. Just before the door closed, he tossed their ladder out on top of them.

"From now on, walk," he growled at them.

The train doors closed and he turned back to Smith with a smile.

"See? Nice and neat."

"You're getting mellow in your old age," Smith said.

"No," Remo said. "Just older."

CHAPTER FOUR

The Secret Service man in the town of Hills was not impressed by Remo's special State Department identification. Remo wondered if he would prefer his Agriculture Department ID, his CIA card, his FBI credentials or his United Nations diplomatic identification, all of which Remo carried because Smith was always giving him credentials that might possibly meet some special set of circumstances, and Remo lost them almost as fast as he was given them.

The older agent took the identification card from Remo's hands and fondled it as if he absorbed information by feel instead of sight.

"Okay, I guess," he said as he handed the card back. "But we already talked to your people today."

"Then you should have your story straight and there shouldn't be any problem in remembering just what happened." He did not like this Agent Derle.

"What happened is easy," Derle said. "We were sitting in our car in front of the train station and Bobby Jack was in the back. Then the Arabs came

50

around the front and said he was gone. We couldn't find him so I guess he was gone."

"You didn't see him go off anywhere?" Remo asked.

"I just said we didn't. You want a beer?"

"No," Remo said. "I'd take some water."

"This house doesn't have water," Derle said. "It's only got beer."

"I'll pass." Remo looked around the living room of Bobby Jack Billings's home. All the furniture was covered with some kind of thick flowered cloth that smelled musty, as if it had been left wet in the bottom of a washing machine for a week.

"What's Billings been like lately?" Remo asked.

Agent Derle sprawled out on one of the couches, across a coffee table from Remo. He shrugged.

"What's he ever like? Up late. Smashed before breakfast. Smashed all day. Smashed at night. Goes to bed."

"He can't be that bad," Remo said.

"That bad? Link's worse than that."

"Why do you call him Link?" Remo asked.

Agent Derle chuckled. "We tell him it's short for Lincoln. He likes that. So does the president."

"It's not short for Lincoln?" Remo asked.

"It's not short for anything. It stands for Link as in Missing Link. That's how he acts. Like some sub-species with a still-evolving bladder."

"He didn't talk about getting lost? Going away? He didn't seem worried about anything?"

"Link doesn't talk about anything except having to go to the bathroom. And the only thing he worries about is running out of beer."

"Where do you think he is?" Remo asked.

Derle shrugged again. "Who knows? It's like you walk down the same street every day and you always see an old gum wrapper on the sidewalk. And then one day the gum wrapper's gone and you say to yourself, what happened to that gum wrapper? But you don't really care. Anything can happen to a gum wrapper."

"You don't sound like you like him much," Remo said. "I thought you guys were supposed to develop emotional attachments to the people you guard."

"Not to Bobby Jack Billings," said Derle.

"All right." Remo stood up. "Where's your partner?"

"He went up to Atlanta for a couple of days to do some work out of the office there. Is that all the questions you have?"

"Yeah."

"You guys are getting easier. The chick today had a lot of questions."

"What chick today?" Remo asked.

"From the State Department too. You must know her. A big six-foot blonde with pigtails and violet eyes. Miss . . . er, Miss Lester."

"Oh, yeah," Remo said. "Her."

"You must have people falling all over yourself," Derle said.

Remo shrugged. "You know how it is," he said.

"Yeah."

"I guess they'll figure maybe I'll find out something she didn't. Two heads are better than one, you know," Remo said.

"Even if one of them's yours?" Derle asked.

"Especially if one of them's mine," Remo said.

He looked at Derle, and his dark eyes burned into the Secret Service agent's, and the agent seemed about to say something, but then he saw deep into the eyes, and what he saw there was something he couldn't put his finger on, so he said nothing, and it was only later that he realized what he had seen. In Remo's eyes, he had had a glimpse of death.

Agent Gavone in Atlanta was no more help to Remo than Derle had been. He didn't think anything was wrong with Billings, had no idea where he might have gone, but he didn't mind talking about Miss Lester who was a lot better looking than Remo.

"Big blonde," he said. "Came up here and asked me a lot of questions. Better questions than you ask."

"Listen," Remo said. He was getting annoyed with comments about his inadequacy. "She just does all my easy advance work. Then I come in to ask about the really important stuff."

"Like what?" Gavone said. "Ask me a really important question."

Remo couldn't think of one. Finally he said, "What kind of beer does Bobby Jack drink?"

"That's important?" Gavone asked.

"You bet it is. It's the key to this whole case," Remo said. "What kind?"

"Any kind."

"He must have a favorite."

"Sure. Whatever's coldest."

"You're not much help," Remo said.

"Ask better questions," said Gavone.

* * *

Mustafa Kaffir was in an upstairs office of the Libyan mission, located in an old mansion in the East Sixties of Manhattan. He listened to a voice coming over a telephone and nodded a lot, but the look on his face was sour and bitter.

He glanced through the second floor window at the New York City police in the street below. It was with wry amusement that he often considered that Libya, whose foreign policy consisted primarily of the slogan "Death to Jews," should have its mission guarded around the clock by police paid for by taxpayers of New York, the city with the largest Jewish population of any city in the world.

He hung up the telephone with a softly muttered "Yes, Colonel," and looked across the office at his assistant. Like Kaffir, he wore traditional Arab robes.

"Trouble, Excellency?" he asked. He was a slim man and he spoke with the casual intimacy common to close friends or lovers, both of which he and Kaffir were.

"It is the lunatic," Kaffir said. "He wishes to mount an armed invasion of Uganda to reinstall Amin on the throne there. Apparently, he has been convinced that the Ugandan people will rise up as one to greet the return of the clown."

His assistant shook his head and pursed his lips.

Kaffir chuckled. "It would be comical if it were not tragic. Can you not see the buffoon now, massing his soldier on the borders of Uganda?" He laughed. "Massing his soldier. Get it?"

"Very funny, Excellency," his assistant said. He

54

had dark eyes and long oiled eyelashes. His skin was light and he looked like an overpainted plaster doll.

"Yeah, very funny," came a voice from the doorway. Kaffir spun in his chair, and saw an American, wearing black trousers and a tee shirt, standing in the door.

"Who . . . ?"

"My name's Remo. I won't need but a couple of minutes of your time. Is it all right to talk in front of this wimp?" He nodded to Kaffir's assistant.

"Who let you up here?" Kaffir said. His assistant reached for the telephone. Remo's hand closed on his, before his hand could close on the phone. The assistant yanked his hand away and massaged it to relieve the pain. It felt as if he had pressed it against a red-hot stove.

"Don't hurt him," Kaffir barked. Remo looked at Kaffir, then at the delicate young man. He understood and nodded.

"I won't hurt him if you cooperate. This will be very quick."

Kaffir hesitated and Remo took a step toward the young assistant, who sank down in his chair, cowering before the American.

"What do you wish to know?" Kaffir said hastily. "Who are you?"

"Who I am isn't important," Remo said. He spoke slowly, choosing his words carefully. "When Bobby Jack Billings wandered away from you the other day, it showed my government that security around the president's family wasn't as good as it could be. Even though we found Bobby Jack and everything's all right, he could just as easily have been kidnapped or harmed. You understand?"

Kaffir nodded. Remo looked to the young assistant who nodded too.

"It's my job to make sure that the security arrangements are improved. So I need your help on that," Remo said. "I have just a few questions."

The questions took only a couple of minutes. Kaffir had seen no one loitering around the train station. He had seen no one drop the medals in the dirt where Bobby Jack Billings had been standing. He had not noticed any unusual behavior on the part of the Secret Service agents.

He finished by saying, "If someone wants to wander off by himself, I guess there is very little way to stop him." He wished, to himself, that Libya's president would wander off by himself. It was certain that no one would stop *him.*

"All right," Remo said. "That's all I needed." He turned back toward the door, but stopped before leaving. "One thing more. Have you been interviewed by an American girl? Tall blonde, hair in braids? Miss Lester?"

"No. I have seen no such woman," Kaffir said.

"You?" Remo asked the assistant.

The young man shook his head.

"Goodbye," Remo said.

They waited long seconds after the door had closed behind Remo before they spoke.

Kaffir said, "They have not yet found the president's brother."

"Apparently not," his assistant said.

"Good," said Kaffir. He reached for the telephone.

"Who are you calling?" his assistant asked.

"Our agent. A warning must be issued," Kaffir said.

president of the United States sat in the Oval
e. He glanced first at his watch, then at his
 secretary, who had arrived to brief him for the
noon press conference that was to begin in fif-
minutes. So that it would not appear wrinkled
levision, the suit jacket the president would
 at the conference was hanging on a coat rack,
 with the fresh, light-blue shirt and dark tie
uld put on at the last moment.
e press secretary was worried. The world had
 from bad to worse. War was ready to break
 the Middle East. Iran, fully anti-American
 had prohibited all shipments of oil to the
.ed States. Gas prices were at an all time high.
lation was churning along in double figures,
ile the economy was turning down and jobless-
ss was soaring. In southern Africa, nationalist
rrillas of liberation, who were supported by the
 e l States against a legally elected government,
 ust killed and mutilated a bus load of mission-
 nd children.
ah, I know all that," the president said, ab-

CHAPTER FIVE

Th
gone
out
now
Unit
Inf
wh
ne
gue
Unit
had
aries
"Ye

ruptly interrupting his assistant. "Is there anything bad happening that they're going to ask me about?"

"Probably nothing but those things," the aide said, his stomach sinking as he spoke. He knew what had happened. Disaster and failure had become so ordinary and commonplace that the president was taking them for granted. It took something more than that to concern the president now.

"Bobby Jack done anything stupid?" the president asked his press secretary. The young man thought the president was watching him a trifle suspiciously.

"No, sir," he said. "Nothing I've heard about anyway."

"The kid ain't done nothin' stupid in school? Wife's behaving herself?"

"Yes, sir.'

"Okay, then, let's get ready to go," the president said. He seemed satisfied, the aide thought, and he only wished that he himself felt that satisfied. The president sometimes seemed to forget that he was in a campaign for reelection, and a faltering economy, stampeding inflation, Middle East war and embarrassments to the government caused by groups the U.S. supported could all make reelection difficult if the press ever decided to write about them.

The president put on his fresh shirt, then slipped the same tie he had been wearing over his head and under the collar of the shirt. He always had trouble tying tie knots, so he tended to use one already-knotted tie as long as he could. He checked his watch one more time, wishing that it would stop and never reach 4 P.M. He hated press conferences. He regarded newsmen as Churchill had once regarded Nazis—always either at your throat or at your feet. If they weren't sucking up to him, trying to get on his good side so they could get exclusive stories, they were trying to trip him up and get him impeached.

He rattled things off in his mind as he slipped on his jacket, adjusted his tie, then walked down the hallway toward the meeting room. Inflation, recession, unemployment, no gas, Iran, terrorists . . . he could handle all that. He had been handling all that every day for the last four years. No surprises there.

He made his opening statement that things were good and getting better and was relieved when none of the reporters laughed. He couldn't remember which reporter had been fed the question to ask about the nation's auto accident fatality rate dropping one one-hundredth of a percentage point, so he just pointed to the first reporter he noticed, a tight-lipped WASP from Chicago who spoke as if his lips were sewn together with surgical thread.

"Thank you, Mr. President," the reporter said when he stood up. "What we'd like to know, sir, is what happened to your hair?"

"I beg your pardon," the president said.

"Your hair. You used to part it on the right side. Now you part it on the left side. Why is that?"

"I always move to the left when a campaign starts," the president said. "Next." He was seething. Of all the stupid questions. With everything happening in the world, that dippy-do wanted to know about his hair? You weren't allowed to change your hairstyle to cover up a receding hairline?

The next reporter wanted to know if the president dyed his hair. No. Was the president going to dye his hair? No. The next reporter wanted to know if the president had ever considered cosmetic surgery. No. Had the First Lady ever considered cosmetic surgery? No.

The next reporter said that two Democratic candidates for some obscure position in Oxnard, California, had called on the party to reject the president and support Bella Abzug for president. The president had no comment. The next questioner wanted to know how many miles a day the president jogged. Five miles. How many miles did the First Lady jog every day? None. She didn't like to jog.

Another reporter stood up, shouting to try to get his question heard over the other reporters shouting questions. When the president looked at him, the other reporters let their questions dribble away into silence.

"Bobby Jack Billings has been noticeable in the last week by his silence, Mr. President," the reporter asked. "Have you muzzled him for the election campaign?"

"Nobody muzzles Bobby Jack," the president said.

He turned to go. Behind him, the obligatory "Thank you, Mr. President" rang out. He walked from the room. Not one question about the economy, taxes, overseas chaos and war in the Middle East. A typical performance, the president thought.

As he stepped into his office, his personal secretary handed him an envelope.

"This just came, sir," she said. "I recognized the handwriting."

So did the president. It was a sprawling scrawl that started somewhere in the top thirty percent of the left hand side of the envelope and dribbled off down to the far right corner. It bore the president's name. The word "President" was misspelled with two s's.

The president thanked his secretary and waited until the door had closed behind her to open the envelope.

The note was from Bobby Jack. There was no mistaking either the semi-literate half-printing that he used in place of handwriting or his use of the president's childhood nickname.

The note read:

Dear Bub. I am held prisoner by some group called PLOTZ. Something about Zionist Terrorists. Won't that be a kick in the ass to all those Jews that hate me? I don't know what they want but they said to tell you I'll be in touch with you later on and don't you go calling the FBI or nothing like that. I am alright.

It was signed "B.J."

The president's press secretary breezed into the office.

"How'd it go, do you think?" the president asked.

"All right," the aide said. "I mean, the assholes want to talk about how you comb your hair." He noticed the president staring at the a piece of paper he held in his hands. "Is everything all right, sir?" he asked.

"Yeah. Fine. Say, did you ever hear of an organization called PLOTZ?"

"PLOTZ with a Z or an S?"

"Z, I guess," the president said. "Something about Zionism."

"Never heard of it," the press secretary said. "Should I check around?"

The president looked at him sharply. "No, no, that won't be necessary." He crumpled up the paper and stuck it into his jacket pocket. "I'm going upstairs to lie down for a while."

"All right, sir."

In his bedroom, the president double-locked the door, then went to the dresser in the far corner of the room. From the back of a bottom drawer, he pulled a red telephone without a dial. He stared at it for twenty seconds, then lifted the receiver.

He knew the telephone would flash in Smith's office. He knew the office was in Rye, New York. But he knew nothing more about it. Was it a luxurious office, or was it as spare and as harsh as Smith himself was over the telephone? He wondered if Smith liked his job. He had worked now for five presidents, and maybe that was proof that Smith liked the work he was doing. For some reason, it seemed important to the president to find that out.

The phone had not completed one buzz when Smith's voice came on the line.

"Yes sir?" he said.

"We've got a little trouble," the president said. "Bobby Jack Bi—"

"I know sir. We're on it," Smith said. "I'm just surprised you took this long to alert us."

"I thought he might just be off drunk somewhere," the president said.

"And now you know he's not?"

The president nodded, then realized that Smith could not see a nod over the telephone. "Yes," he said. "I just got a note from him."

"All right," Smith said. "Read it to me."

After the president had read the note, Smith said, "Thank you. We'll continue our investigation." The next thing he would hear would be the click of the telephone in his ear as Smith hung up, the president knew.

"Hold on," he said rapidly. "Just a minute."

There was silence on the other end of the phone. Then Smith said, "Yes, sir?"

"Tell me. Do you like your job?" the president asked.

"Like it?" Smith repeated.

"That's right. Do you like it? Do you like your work?"

There was another brief silence before Smith said, "I have never given it any thought, sir. I don't know." And this time the president had no chance to say any more before the telephone cut off in his ear.

Remo telephoned Smith from a sidewalk telephone booth near Central Park in New York. Chiun remained behind in the car which was illegally parked at the curb on Fifth Avenue.

"The Libyans don't know anything," Remo reported.

Smith said, "The president has gotten a note from Bobby Jack."

"What's it say?"

"It says that he's being held prisoner by some group called PLOTZ. Something about Zionists."

"PLOTZ?" Remo said. "You're kidding."

"No. PLOTZ."

"Who are they?" Remo asked.

"I don't know. There's nothing in the tapes. I'm trying to find out who they might be."

"You think this PLOTZ has anything to do with the Star of David and the swastika that were found?" Remo asked.

He could sense Smith's shrug of "who knows" over the telephone. Finally Smith said, "At least it clears up one thing. The president didn't have anything to do with Billings being stolen away. Otherwise he would have just tried to keep us in the dark."

"Good," Remo said. "I've got a question. Who is a Miss Lester from the State Department? I keep tripping over her."

"Hold on," Smith said. Remo rested the telephone on his shoulder. He knew Smith was punching up the television console on his desk and feeding the Lester name into it. Remo looked out over Central Park. It had once been a glorious urban park, but now it was generally safe to use the park only between noon and three P.M., if you were traveling with an armed escort.

Smith's voice crackled over the phone.

"Do you have a physical description of this woman?"

"Tall. Almost six feet. Blonde, hair in braids. Violet eyes," Remo said.

"Hold on." Remo looked toward the car parked at the curb. Chiun's eyes were closed in repose.

"Negative," said Smith. "Nobody like that in our

State Department, and nobody by that name or description in our file of U.S. agents."

"Good," Remo said.

"Why good?"

"Because she's the only lead we've got."

"Not much of a lead," Smith said. "She seems to be looking for him too."

"Details," Remo said airily. "Just details. At least she knows he's missing. She found that out somewhere, and that's something for us to work on. Let me know when you find out something about PLOTZ. PLOTZ . . . hah."

CHAPTER SIX

As Remo came into their hotel room overlooking Central Park in New York, Chiun was turning off the television set. He turned toward Remo, his face alight with excitement.

"I have decided," he said, "what I am going to do next."

"Good," said Remo. He flopped down on a sofa. He lay with the top of his head toward Chiun. Perhaps if Chiun could not see his eyes, Chiun would not talk to him.

Chiun walked down toward Remo's feet and stared into Remo's eyes.

"Do you not wish to know what I am going to do?" he asked. He carefully scrutinized Remo's face for reaction.

"Of course I do," Remo said. He wondered what Chiun had seen on television this time that had set him off.

"I am going to the Olympic Games," Chiun said. "I'm going for the gold."

"That's fine," Remo said, "except they don't have an event for assassins."

70

"Foolish child," Chiun said. "I will not go as an assassin."

"What will you go as?"

"Everything else," Chiun said.

"I beg your pardon," Remo said.

"You're excused. I will go as everything else. I have been watching this television all day, and I have watched these people running around and jumping and using poles and lifting weights and throwing spears and lumps of iron and I can do those things better than these people. So I am going. That is that."

Remo sat up on the couch. Chiun sat on the floor in front of him.

"Why?" Remo said. "You know you can do those things and I know you can do those things, so why go?"

"I want everybody to know I can do those things."

"I thought you told me once that knowing your own virtue is enough recognition for the thinking man," Remo said.

"Forget I said that," Chiun replied. He folded his arms across the chest. His long-fingernailed hands disappeared in the voluminous sleeves of his white silk kimono. "I am going."

Remo looked at him. He had no doubt, not even for an instant, that in any event Chiun would eat the Olympic medalists alive. But why all of a sudden this urge for public recognition?

"What do you get out of it?" Remo asked.

"Endorsements," Chiun said. "Eat Wheato cereal, the breakfast of Chiun, the champion. Chiun, the champion, runs on Tigerpaw sneakers. Chiun, the

71

champion, stays well dressed in shirts by Sanford. I have seen this, Remo. Even people who do nothing but swim get these endorsements and they go on television, looking silly, and get great amounts of money to say such things."

"But you don't eat Wheato Cereal, and you don't even wear sneakers, much less Tigerpaw sneakers. Shirts by Sanford? I've never seen you wear anything but a kimono."

"So I'll lie a little. Everybody does. You know very well that no one ever made it to the Olympics by eating Wheato Cereal. Anyone eating that would be lucky to survive, much less run a race."

"You don't need the money," Remo said.

"One never knows," Chiun said. "I'm not getting any younger. The money from endorsements might help insure my old age."

"Back in Sinanju, you've got a houseful of gold and jewels. You don't need the money," Remo insisted stubbornly.

"And suppose I get sick and all my life's savings are eaten away by doctor bills," Chiun said.

"You've never been sick a day in your life," Remo answered.

Chiun raised his right index finger and shook it at Remo. "Aaaah," he said, "that's just the point. I am overdue."

Remo lay back on the sofa. It was all Smith needed to make him absolutely bananas. Chiun going to the Olympic games. Chiun being interviewed in the press tent after each winning event. Crediting his victories to clean living, good eating, and the support he had received from Dr. Harold

W. Smith, head of the secret agency CURE, for which Chiun helped kill America's enemies.

Remo rolled on his side to look at Chiun.

"Who will you represent?"

"What do you mean?"

"Every athlete comes from somewhere. They represent somebody or something. Some country. You come from North Korea. You want to represent them?"

"No," Chiun said. "No television in North Korea. No endorsement money. I will represent the United States."

"Oh," Remo said. He rolled over again onto his back and stared at the ceiling. Chiun began to hum the Olympic anthem, which he must have heard on television that afternoon.

"I think you have to be a citizen of the country you represent," Remo finally said.

"I don't think so," Chiun said, "but if you do, I'll lie."

"Oh," Remo said. Back to staring at the ceiling. Chiun resumed humming. Remo glanced at him out of the corner of his eye. He was practicing bowing his head, so that the Olympic gold medals could be slipped around his neck.

Remo lay in silence for a long time. Then he thought of it. He sat up on the sofa. Chiun stopped humming and looked at him.

"You can't do it, Chiun."

"Why not?"

"Because of the Olympic uniforms."

"What does that mean?"

"You have to wear shorts and tights and bare legs

to compete in the Olympics," Remo said. He pointed toward the television. "Like everybody you see. You don't see anybody competing in a kimono."

Chiun's face clouded over. "Is this true?" he asked. There was hurt in his voice, and Remo knew why. Chiun had an ancient Oriental distaste for exposing his body. He bathed in private behind double-locked doors. When he changed from one kimono to another, he did it in such a way that his body was never visible. He represented centuries of modesty.

"I'm afraid it is, " Remo said. "You know how it is. In some events, they have to judge you on style, and that means how you hold your legs, and how correctly pointed your toes are and like that. They just couldn't judge you wearing a kimono."

The telephone rang. Remo got up to answer it.

Chiun restrained him with a hand on Remo's shoulder.

"You are not just saying this?"

"Think about it," Remo said. "On television, all those athletes are wearing shorts." He shrugged. "Sorry, Chiun, looks like you've been scratched."

Chiun's face twisted in anger. The telephone rang again. "That is a supid rule you have," Chiun snarled. He moved from the room like a puff of smoke through an exhaust fan. The door shivered on its hinges as it slammed behind him.

Remo picked up the telephone. It was Smith.

"I've found PLOTZ," Smith said.

"Good," Remo said. "Where?"

"You're not going to believe this,' Smith said.

"Believe what?"

74

"They just bought a loft building in Hoboken, New Jersey."

"How'd you find that out?" Remo asked.

"They bought it under their own name," Smith said. "It turned up on the records in the county registrar's office. Building purchased by the Pan-Latin Organization against Terrorist Zionism."

"That's not exactly being secretive, is it?" Remo asked.

"They've also applied for a federal tax exemption as a non-profit corporation," Smith said.

"You're right. I don't believe it," Remo said.

"And try this. They've sent out a press release to announce their formation and their schedule of activities for the next month."

"Wait a minute now," Remo said. "A terrorist group that kidnaps the president's brother-in-law is going public?"

"That's what it looks like," Smith said.

"They ain't wrapped too tight."

Chiun came back into the room as Smith said, "I have all the information here. Write it down.'

Remo looked on the end table for a pencil.

"Hold on, Smitty," he said. He looked over at Chiun who stood near the desk of the hotel room.

"Chiun," he said.

The old man slowly turned his head to look at Remo.

"Give me a pen out of that drawer, will you?"

Chiun folded his arms.

"C'mon, Chiun, stop fooling around."

"Look for your own pen."

"I need to write down a number."

"What is the number?" Chiun asked.

"Smitty, what's the address?"

"One-eleven Water Street, Hoboken," Smith said.

"One-eleven Water Street, Hoboken," Remo told Chiun.

"Now you no longer have any need to write it down," Chiun said. "You will remember it forever."

"No, I won't. I'll forget it."

"You will remember it. I guarantee it," Chiun said.

"All right," Remo growled. "I'll fix you. One-eleven Water Street and I'm going to forget it as soon as I hang up."

"Remo," Smith's voice crackled into the phone.

"Yeah, Smitty."

"What are you doing?"

"Never mind. What's the name of the person with this organization?"

"Freddy Zentz," Smith said.

"Chiun," Remo called. "Remember Freddy Zentz."

"Never," Chiun said. "Remember it yourself." Remo saw Chiun's hands busy in the drawer of the desk.

"I've got it, Smitty," Remo said. "Freddy Zentz, PLOTZ, One-eleven Water Street, Hoboken."

"Get right on it," Smith said. "Goodbye."

Remo hung up and went to the desk drawer. Chiun moved aside to make room for him.

Inside the drawer, Remo found the hotel's complimentary pen. It had been snapped in half.

"You're really not a nice person, Chiun," said Remo.

"When I win the Olympic gold, then I will have

time to be a nice person," Chiun said. "If people stop putting roadblocks in my way."

"Aaaaah," Remo snarled. "Try this. Freddy Zentz, PLOTZ, One-eleven Water Street, Hoboken. How do you like that?"

"Congratulations," said Chiun. "The joy of victory instead of the agony of defeat."

Remo hummed the Olympic anthem, and Chiun left the room.

Remo remembered Hoboken. It was a tight little town, only about a mile square, and when he had been with the Newark Police Department he had often gone to a restaurant on River Street, where he had stood at the bar with a lot of other men eating raw clams and throwing the shells on the floor. It was a famous men's bar and this was a custom that dated back to the nineteenth century. Then some women had sued, claiming an all-man's bar was a violation of their civil rights. The bar owners had fought in court but they had lost. The women came to the bar like avenging Valkyries. Within two days, they were complaining about the clam shells on the floor because they kept losing their balance when they stepped on shells in their high heels. Remo stopped going.

When he drove into Hoboken and turned on River Street, he felt a pinch of nostalgia as he passed the bar and restaurant. Life had been simpler in those days, but so had he. His body had been just a normal man's body, somehow managing to struggle through life. That was before Chiun had taught him that the average person used less than ten percent of his body's potential, and had shown Remo how to move up his percentages. The number for Remo now was fifty percent and climbing. Chiun told him that the only acceptable figure was 100 percent. The only 100 percenter in the world was frail, aged Chiun. That was one thing that Chiun had taught him. Another was that raw clams were mucus and no man should eat mucus and Remo realized with regret that he would never again eat another raw clam.

He turned toward the Hudson River. He had no trouble finding the loft building at One-eleven Water Street, because there was a crowd of young children milling around outside. As Remo parked the car, he saw a sign strung between the second-floor windows of the building: PAN-LATIN ORGAN-IZATION AGAINST TERRORIST ZIONISM.

A smaller sign imparted the information that the children had come to PLOTZ headquarters for a Meet-Your-Terrorist open house, at which they had been promised free hot dogs. The children were chewing on hot dogs wrapped in yellow napkins with printing on them.

Chiun asked Remo as they approached the building, "Are all these children poor and starving? Is this the seamy underside of America?"

"No," Remo said. "Kids'll eat anything."

As he walked up the steps, he filched one of the napkins from under a child's frankfurter.

"How to make your own Molotov cocktail," the napkin said, and showed with drawings and simple text how to make a gasoline bottle bomb.

"Nice folks," Remo mumbled.

They were met at the top of the steps by a tall woman handing out hot dogs from a large black metal pot. She wore a bandanna around her head, and large, circular-lensed eyeglasses, tinted violet. The glasses were so large that Remo thought they made her look like a praying mantis. A beautiful praying mantis, but a praying mantis nevertheless. She wore blue jeans and a plaid shirt and her face was lightly tanned, but it was still smooth with none of the lines and wrinkles women get when they insist upon converting facial skin into leather.

She placed a hot dog in Remo's hand. He turned and handed it to a child.

"No thanks," he said. "I already know how to make a bomb."

The young woman shrugged. "You never know, your memory might fail you." With a small smile, she reached out to place a hot dog in Chiun's hand. The old Oriental looked at her in disgust and folded his hands together inside the sleeves of his orange kimono.

"The frankfurters are really quite good," she said. "Even if you don't like the commercial that comes with it, the food is wholesome." Her accent was not quite American, Remo thought, but then neither was a Hoboken accent. Still, this wasn't a Hoboken accent. People often confused a New Jersey accent with a Brooklyn accent, but there was really little comparison. Brooklyn mispronounced certain syllables; New Jersey just ignored them.

"Wholesome?" said Chiun. "Pork?"

"All beef," the woman said. "We have to answer to a higher authority."

"That is worse," said Chiun, "for if there is anything more disgusting than eating pig, it is eating cow."

"Well, if you're not here for the food, why are you here?" the woman asked.

"We're looking for . . ." Remo paused. "What's his name, Chiun?"

"Think of it yourself," Chiun said.

"Freddy Zentz?" the woman asked Remo.

"That's it," he said. "But you didn't have to say it. I would have thought of it. Freddy Zentz. We want to sign up for the revolution."

The woman kept spearing hot dogs from the black pot and slapping them onto rolls as she spoke with Remo.

"And what police agency are you with?" she asked.

"My, my, aren't we suspicious?" Remo said. "Do we look like cops?"

"He doesn't," the woman told Remo. "You might."

"Honest," Remo said. "Not me. My friend here is one of the world's great blower-ups of automobiles. Me, I'm just a talented amateur but I learn fast."

"My name's Jessica," the woman said. She nodded to a girl, a twelve-year-old with braces and pigtails, and the girl moved into place behind the black pot to start handing out food.

"Come on inside," the woman told Remo. "We'll see if Freddy's around."

The interior of the loft building was a blessed relief from the din and clamor of the children on the steps. Remo and Chiun stood with Jessica in a large room. Its walls were covered with posters.

Remo was happy to see that clenched fists had retained their drawing power. There were also a string of posters done in the traditional Communist art style in which a man and a woman, side by side, looked bravely off into a future which resumably was going to provide them all with necks, a feature they did not now have.

Other posters showed large Stars of David with black X's drawn through them, and several were actually blow-ups of printed instructions on making various kinds of bombs.

"I'll find Freddy," Jessica said. She stood close to Remo and met him eye to eye. "Wait here." She padded off silently and Remo noticed that she was barefoot.

"Hello," he said. He recognized the voice immediately. He listened for a moment, then said, "So they've introduced a resolution that all NATO countries should disarm. What about it?"

He listened for a moment, then sputtered, "What do you mean, you're thinking of voting for it?"

Pause.

"No, Andy. You've got it wrong again. Now think about it this way. We're the good guys. They're the bad guys . . . I know they're not all bad guys . . . but think about it that way."

Pause.

"No, no. The Communists . . . they're against us. What do you want to take their side for?"

Pause.

"No, no. Let's go slow. See, let me try to explain it to you, real simple like. There's two forces in the world, see. Us and them. We are for freedom. They are for Communism."

Pause.

"No, Andy. We don't want to attack freedom. We are for Communism."

Pause.

"I don't care if they're nice people to talk to. They're trying to destroy our country."

Pause.

"No, it wouldn't be a good thing if they destroyed our country, even if you do think we're all racists. It's not going to get any better if they conquer the world."

Pause.

"I know they say it'll be better if they conquer the world, but do you believe them?"

Pause.

"Oh, you do."

Pause.

"I know you never hear about people being oppressed in those countries. That's because they send people who oppose them away to slave camps or insane asylums and nobody hears from them again."

Pause.

"Honest, Andy, that's true. No, it's not just capitalist propaganda. It's really true."

Pause.

"I know because our intelligence people tell us."

Pause.

"In this case, you really can believe them because they're telling the truth. Now, you got it right?"

Pause.

"Let's hear it."

"No, no. You got it wrong again. See, it's like a cowboy movie. The good guys and the bad guys. We wear the white hats and they wear the black hats."

Pause.

"I know you don't wear hats. It's just a figure of speech. Dammit, just vote *no*."

The president slammed the telephone receiver down. Again before he could leave his desk, it rang again and when he heard the voice, his eyes rolled upward in his head.

"That's right. I said, vote no. N-O. No. That's right. I don't care if it does make the Third World mad at us."

This time, he hung up, then quickly laid the

phone on its side on the desk. Anybody calling now would get just a busy signal.

He told his secretary that he was going upstairs to lie down. The secretary welcomed the idea; the president seemed to be under a lot of strain lately.

In his bedroom, the president removed the red CURE telephone from the dresser drawer. Smith answered immediately.

"Yes, Mr. President."

The president outlined the newest note and Smith said, "I should have the originals of both notes." He told the president to have the messages helicoptered into Westchester County Airport in White Plains. Smith would have them picked up there.

"How are you doing so far?" the president asked.

"Nothing to report yet, sir," Smith said.

"I've decided if something doesn't happen soon, I'm going to announce that Bobby Jack's missing."

"I think that would be a mistake," Smith said. "Right now, you are getting messages from him and he is presumably alive. If you upset the balance, he may wind up dead. I think it would be a mistake. Also, you may well have every lunatic in the country claiming credit for the kidnapping."

"Credit isn't exactly the word I would have used," the president said.

"Responsibility, then," Smith said. "All our resources would be strained trying to check out the false leads."

"I'll think about it," the president said. "Please keep me advised. The helicopter will be there in two hours."

He replaced the telephone in the back of the dresser drawer and lay down upon the bed.

There were a lot of judgments to be made, judgments on which course of action would be safer for Bobby Jack's life. But there was also a political judgment. Would announcing Bobby Jack's kidnapping be politically good or bad? Maybe a grieving friend might be worth something in the popularity polls. But, on the other hand, people might say that the president was so inept he couldn't even protect his own family from kidnappers; how was he going to protect America?

He tried to put it out of his mind and fell asleep hoping that Andy would remember to vote *no*.

CHAPTER EIGHT

Remo and Chiun sat with six other men in the living room at One-eleven Water Street, waiting for Freddy Zentz, the titular head of PLOTZ, to make his appearance. Jessica, the tall girl from the hot dog pot, was in and out of the room.

Remo looked at the other six men. They were wearing shorts or tie-dyed jeans or chinos, and tee shirts with marijuana drawings on them, and sweatshirts that read "Property of Alcatraz—Unlisted Number." But they didn't ring true; something didn't fit the terrorist mold. Perhaps it was their age. The youngest of the men was thirty, the oldest pushing fifty.

Freddy Zentz arrived just after 8 P.M. Remo thought he looked like the head clerk at a Philadelphia race track. He wore a powder-blue polyester leisure suit and white plastic patent leather shoes. Remo wondered if every man in America owned a blue leisure suit. Zentz was a small, slight man. Surprisingly, he had a closed-cropped haircut. He wore thick horn-rimmed eyeglasses and was missing his two canine teeth, so that when he smiled, as he did in greeting, he looked like a beaver approaching a succulent birch tree. He was about thirty.

"Hello, hello, hello," he said. Solemnly he walked around the room shaking hands with each of them in turn. Jessica stayed behind in the doorway to the room, smiling maternally, as if this were her son with whom she was well pleased.

"Welcome to the wonderful world of the Pan-Latin Organization against Terrorist Zionism," Freddy said to each of them in turn, as his thin bony hand shot from his sleeve like an unleashed piston. Remo shook his hand and restrained his impulse to crush his bones. Chiun listened to Zentz's greeting without expression on his face. But he kept his hands inside his kimono sleeves, and when it appeared that Zentz might stand in front of him all night waiting for Chiun to shake his hand, Chiun closed his eyes, signaling clearly that the audience was ended.

When he was done making the rounds of the room, Zentz pulled a chair to the front wall, near the old unworkable fireplace.

"I'm glad you all came," he said. "I was hoping for more, but this is a pretty good nucleus." He pronounced the word "nook-a-luss." Jessica sat down on the floor in the doorway at the other end of the room. She looked at Remo, who smiled at her. She smiled back.

Remo wanted to ask what the organization was all about.

A man across the room from Remo with a face that was cragged and riven said to Zentz, "What's this organization all about?"

Zentz's eyes twinkled with satisfaction. "What

you have the privilege of being in on is the first wave of the new wave of revolutionary action." He paused as if that had answered the question.

Remo was going to ask what that meant when another man at the end of the room near Zentz asked, "What does that mean?"

"It means that the Pan-Latin Organization against Terrorist Zionism is a new kind of information house for groups that understand the basic corruption of the United States and all its allies around the world, preying as they do on the poor and the weak, so that the big money industrialists and the robber baron oil companies and all those who partake of America's racist fare can grow sleek and fat."

Remo noticed the expressions around the room ranged from distaste to disgust. Except Chiun, whose eyes were still closed and his face impassive, and Jessica who seemed enraptured by all the truth and beauty that Zentz was revealing.

Remo was going to press the question again, but someone beat him to it.

"Yeah," the man asked from his seat next to Remo. "But what does that mean? Against Terrorist Zionism. Does that mean we're against the Jews and for the Arabs or what? What does that mean?"

"We are against everybody who is against freedom for the masses," Freddy Zentz said. Jessica squealed a little and clapped her hands together in appreciation. A dip, Remo thought. An absolute dip. Zentz favored her with a slight nod of appreciation for her applause.

Remo was going to ask who decided what countries were against freedom for the masses, when a fat man across the room, obscenely dressed in an Indian style pull-over shirt and blue and white blotched, bleached jeans, asked that same question.

"As your leader, I do," said Freddy Zentz.

The fat man persisted. "Okay, then what do we do about it all?"

Everybody's attention riveted sharply on Zentz.

And then it hit Remo. There was something unusual about the other men in the room: they were all cops. He hadn't noticed it before, but like cops everywhere, no matter what their disguises, they were wearing heavy thick-soled shoes. And they all wore wristwatches, and all the watches had leather bands. All cops and all sitting there, on assignment from whatever departments they represented, waiting for Zentz to say enough to hang himself.

Zentz had cleared his throat. "You ask what we do about it all," he said.

"That's right. That's what I asked," the fat man said. Now that he knew they were all cops, Remo wondered where this man came from. The fat man probably was a Hoboken cop. No one else would try to dress a 250-pound man with a bald spot in jeans and pass him off as a hippie. Maybe a Hell's Angel, but not a hippie. Particularly since Remo could see the bottom of a tattooed ship's anchor peeking out from under the cuff of his open sleeve.

"Too often in the past," Zentz said, "terrorist groups have tried to take the law into their own hands. They've gone to the street with bombs and guns, as if that way they could convince people of the rightness of their cause. And all they did was to get the public mad at them. They gave terrorism a bad name. We're doing something new." He looked

93

around the room as if expecting a standing ovation. Instead he got six men who asked simultaneously: "What?"

"We're not going to be a field organization," said Zentz. "That way we're going to stay legal, 'cause the last thing in the world we need is a lot of dim-witted cops stomping around here with their big feet trying to arrest us on trumped-up charges." Remo noticed the six other men in the room pull their heavily clad feet back farther under their chairs. He saw six pairs of tightly set lips and realized that if Zentz were ever booked for anything, he had just cleverly arranged for the charge to be upgraded to a capital offense. Zentz, however, realized no such thing. He was still pouring it on.

"We're going to be a clearing house for information," he said. "Instead of going out on the street and setting off bombs, which always gets the public pissed at you, we're going to convince other people to set the bombs off."

"That's still a crime," one of the men said. "Inciting to violence or riot or something."

"Bullshit," said Zentz. "That's free speech. Nobody ain't gonna tell me what to say." He had gotten agitated as he answered the question and with his two solitary front teeth dipping up and down, he looked like a mouse working over a wedge of imported Swiss cheese.

His next sentence was overpowered by a loud thump out in the street. The other men in the room looked startled, but Zentz smiled.

"There," he said. "The first fruits of our labors. All children need is someone to guide them." Remo thought back to the afternoon and the instruction sheets for making Molotov cocktails which were printed on the hot dog napkins PLOTZ had distributed to the children.

There was another thump out in the street and another. Remo noticed Chiun had opened his eyes. His cold hazel eyes were staring at Zentz now.

"Should we all go see what's going on?" Zentz said. He rose to his feet. Chiun was up also.

"Yes," Chiun said. "We must see just what you are responsible for."

Remo stood up alongside Chiun. He knew the age-old prohibition of the House of Sinanju against involving children in the theater of death.

The men trailed out onto the steps of the building behind Zentz. As they stood on the sidewalk, there was a roar and a flash of heat enveloped them. A car had been burning half a block away, ignited by a Molotov cocktail, and the flames had finally reached its gas tank, which exploded.

Drops of gasoline had splattered into the air and dropped down on other cars, igniting the paint. Some of the gasoline had set afire summer-dried bushes in front of a few of the old frame houses. The sound of oncoming fire engines could be heard, their klaxon horns whooping in the evening stillness. A group of young children, none more than 12 years old, stood across from the fire scene, shouting exultantly.

"Dynamite," said Zentz. "Great. Marvelous." He turned around and looked at the other men's faces. "Ain't that something?" he said. Remo looked around at the men whose faces were set tight in anger. He noticed that Jessica had not joined them.

"Let's go look for some more," Zentz said. He marched off with the men trailing him. Chiun walked at his side.

"You like this?" Chiun asked.

"Great. First we train the kids, and they'll bring this government down."

"With fires and death?" Chiun asked.

"Whatever it takes," Zentz said.

Remo moved up alongside the two other men. "This is all good," he said, "but we ought to maybe do something more dramatic." He spoke softly so he was not overheard by the six policemen who were following them. "Like kidnap somebody. Say, like Bobby Jack Billings." He looked at Zentz's face for some reaction.

The reaction was a scowl. "Naaah," said Zentz. "That kind of stuff gets you into trouble. Feds and all that bullshit, breaking laws. I like what we're doing."

"Is there anybody else in this organization but you?" Remo asked. "I like to know who I'm joining."

"Not yet, maybe," Zentz said. "But someday we'll have an army. You can see what these kids can do. Wait until we have thousands."

"It will never happen for you," Chiun said grimly.

They turned the corner and looked up Fourth Street toward Washington Street, the city's main thoroughfare. Four cars had been ignited and were burning. Sparks had started a fire in the dry wood siding of a four-story frame house near the cars.

"Swell," said Zentz. "Marvelous. Great."

"Sick," said Chiun.

"Who puts up the money for this organization?" Remo asked Zentz.

"Public donations," the young man said. He was rubbing his hands together in gleeful satisfaction as he looked at the fires. "I love fires," he said. "There's something pure about them. Clean."

"You think so?" Chiun said. He saw another group of children standing across the street from the fire scene. They were twenty feet ahead now of the other six men.

"Yeah. Don't you think so?" Zentz said. "Just look at those flames."

"If you enjoy them so much . . ." Chiun said.

Before Remo could reach out a hand to stop him, Chiun had grasped Zentz's right wrist. He twirled the man around in front of him like a stone on a string, then let him go. Feet first, Zentz went through the brittle back window of a burning car. His body vanished inside the car. His screams filled the night. He tried to climb up through the same broken window. Just as he did, the flames reached the car's gas tank.

It exploded. The roar muffled Zentz's screams, and when the first flash of flame had lessened, there was no longer any sign of the PLOTZ director in the window.

Remo sighed. "You're getting pretty goddamn dangerous around cars," he said.

"Somebody who loves fire that much should not be deprived of his enjoyment," Chiun said.

"I was still questioning him about PLOTZ," Remo said.

"The fool knew nothing. Questions were a waste of time."

The six men came running up behind them.

"Was that him in the car?" the fat man with the balding head said.

"Yeah," Remo said. "What department you with?"

"Hoboken police," the man said. He looked at the burning car. "Good riddance to bad rubbish."

The other five men stood around.

"It looked like he jumped into that car," one of them said.

"He did," Remo said. "My friend here tried to stop him, but he just shook him off."

"Shit," another man said. "I'll be up all night writing reports on this."

They turned out to be from the Hoboken police, the New Jersey police, the FBI, the county prosecutor's office, the county sheriff's office, and the U.S. Attorney General's office.

Remo and Chiun left them on the corner by the car, concocting a plan whereby only one of them would have to write a report, and the others could all file duplicates. Since policemen hated writing reports worse than they hated crime, this idea appealed to all of them.

"C'mon," Remo said. "We'll get back and see what's in Zentz's office."

As they ran to the front of the loft building, a yellow cab was pulling away from the curb. They hurried inside the building. Zentz's office door was open; so was his safe and his filing cabinets. Papers had been riffled, and files had been yanked.

"That woman," Remo said.

"Correct," said Chiun.

"She's taken the files."

"Correct and obvious," Chiun answered.

"We've got to get her," Remo said.

"Whatever makes you happy," Chiun replied.

They ran back out of the building toward their rented car, parked a block away.

As Remo unlocked the door and started inside, Chiun said, "You are going to drive this car?"

"Of course," Remo said. "I drove it here, didn't I?" He reached across and unlocked the door for Chiun who slid in onto the front seat next to Remo.

Remo started the engine which caught with a smooth purr.

"Where are we going?" Chiun asked.

"I hadn't thought of that," Remo said.

"Think of it," Chiun said.

Remo thought of it. "Newark Airport. It's right near here. If that chick is splitting by cab, that's probably where she went." He nodded his head, agreeing with himself.

Remo dropped the gear shift into drive and pulled away from the curb.

Kerthunk. Kerthunk. Kerthunk.

"What the hell is that?" asked Remo.

"Four tires that are no longer round," Chiun said.

"Four flats?" Remo said.

Chiun nodded.

"She flattened our tires so we couldn't follow her," Remo said.

"Don't whine," Chiun said. "It is not becoming to you."

Remo nosed the car into a parking spot and turned off the engine. With Chiun behind him, he ran up the block. At the corner of First Street, they saw a yellow cab and jumped into the back seat.

The cab was obviously the pride of the Hoboken

fleet in that it had one wheel on each corner and still had all its fenders. This was no mean feat in a city in which the police regularly announced crack-downs on triple parking along Washington Street, the city's main thoroughfare, a street that was a hundred feet wide but so snarled by parked cars that getting through it on anything wider than a bicycle tested the endurance of man and the permanence of steel.

The driver looked at them.

"I'm supposed to be going home now," he said.

"Newark Airport. Then you go home," Remo said.

"Naah," the driver said. "Gotta go home now."

Remo put his hand on the vinyl seat cover of the seat next to the driver. He closed his fingers and ripped out a large chunk of vinyl and foam rubber, exposing the seat's steel springs.

The driver looked at Remo, the ripped seat, and then at Remo again.

He shook his head and screeched from the curb.

"Newark Airport coming up."

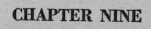

CHAPTER NINE

When the cost of building the Lincoln and Holland Tunnels under the Hudson River was repaid, the Port Authority of New York and New Jersey was supposed to make the two conduits toll-free. However, the Port Authority always managed to find a way to avoid such displays of public largesse. It built the tunnels and kept the fares intact. Then it built some more, and raised the tunnel fares for motorists—even though the cost of the tunnels had been paid by tolls five times over.

One of its projects was the rebuilding of Newark Airport. The Port Authority had built the airport four times as large as it had to be. This surplus of space and network of only partially used roads made the airport the most efficient, the easiest to get into and out of, of any airport in the continental United States.

Remo and Chiun's taxi fare from Hoboken was fourteen dollars and fifty cents. Remo paid with a twenty and told the driver to keep the change.

Chiun said this was wasteful. "If he is supposed to get twenty dollars, that little box there should say twenty dollars. Why do you give him twenty dollars when the little box says fourteen dollars?"

"That's a tip. It's an American custom," Remo said.

"What is?"

"To pay somebody extra for good service."

"Do you pay less for bad service?" Chiun asked.

"No."

"Then you are an idiot. Get your change."

This conversation took place in the back seat of the cab. The driver, who did not have the latest New York City inventions—bullet-proof electrified glass partitions that separated him from his passengers, and alarm lights and bells on top of the cab that could be seen from four miles away and heard from halfway around the world—leaned over his back seat and paid attention. He was rooting for Remo.

He nodded approvingly as Remo told Chiun, "No, I don't want the change."

"I do," said Chiun. He looked at the driver. "Change, please."

The driver shook his head. "It's an American custom, fella. Listen to your friend there. He's telling you right. Good drivers like me always get a tip. A little something extra."

"You want something extra?" Chiun said.

The driver nodded.

Chiun grabbed the back of the front seat, his hands on each side of the gouge Remo had taken from the vinyl and foam. The old Oriental wrenched with his hands, gently. Two more big rips of material came from the seat. Chiun opened the door and stepped outside onto the sidewalk.

Behind him, Remo gave the driver two more twenties. "Fix your seat," he said.

On the sidewalk, he said to Chiun, "You're in a fine mood."

"It is your fault for making me meet that creature who makes children into criminals. It spoiled my night."

"It didn't do much for his either," Remo said.

As they walked to the automatic terminal doors, a black car pulled up at curbside behind their taxi cab. Two men in dark blue business suits got out.

As they passed through the doors, Chiun asked Remo, "Are you aware?"

Without turning, Remo said, "Yeah. Two of them. This might be a break."

Chiun nodded. He and Remo walked off toward the south end of the terminal, moving slowly, waiting until they were sure the two men from the black car had not lost view of them.

"I know what you're so ticked about," Remo said. Chiun was silent. "You're just upset 'cause I won't ask Smitty to send you to the Olympic games."

"It is all right," Chiun said. "I am working on an alternative."

They went up an escalator. As they were stepping off, Remo felt under his feet the weight of two men stepping on the escalator below them.

They turned to the left. Ahead, Remo saw a door marked "no admittance." He and Chiun moved quickly inside. Remo saw it was a room used for record-keeping by the baggage handling staff. It was empty of workers.

Remo held the door open long enough for their two pursuers to get off the escalator and follow them. Then he let the door swing closed. He moved against the far wall of the room and told Chiun, "Now behave yourself."

"I will not lift a finger," Chiun said. He looked out the window and folded his arms.

The two men came into the room, their hands in their pockets, obviously holding guns.

They were startled when they saw Chiun with his back to them and Remo leaning against a wall casually, as if waiting for them.

"Come on in," Remo said. "Plenty of room for you too. Don't be shy."

The two men were swarthy with dark hair and thin mustaches. One smiled as the door closed tightly behind them. Both men withdrew their hands from their pockets. Heavy automatics were cradled in their fists.

"All right," Remo said. "Now who are you? You better talk, before I unleash my friend here."

The two men smiled. Chiun remained with his back to the room.

"It is not who we are," one said with a thick accent that Remo had heard very recently. "It is who you are."

"Oh, us," Remo said. "I'm Remo. This is Chiun. We're secret agents for the United States government. Now who are you?"

"We are representatives of—" one man begun.

"Ahmir," the other spoke sharply, interrupting him and cautioning him to silence.

"That's your last word on the subject?" Remo said.

"The last word you will ever hear," the man said. He leveled his automatic at Remo's chest. The other man aimed his weapon at Chiun's unmoving back.

"Chiun, are you going to stop fooling around?" Remo said.

Chiun raised his arms over his head in a motion that suggested Remo get lost. Remo shook his head. He watched the men's hands. He was nine feet away from them. The one aimed at Chiun showed tension in his trigger finger. The other's index finger was still loosely held inside the trigger guard. As Remo watched, the trigger finger on the weapon aimed at Chiun tightened.

Remo made a movement to the right, a sudden curl of his body that forced his man to swing his gun to the side, and squeeze off a shot at him. But even before the shot had been fired, Remo was moving back left, diving through the air, his body parallel to the floor. His hand closed on the weapon aimed at Chiun just as the trigger was depressed, but the bullet fired harmlessly into the floor. The second man had swung around, again aiming at Remo, but this time, before he could get off a shot, Remo's right foot lashed out. The tip of his right toe caught the underside of the weapon and drove it around and upward so that it plunged barrel-first into the gunman's throat. The man's eyes opened saucer wide, and then, as Remo watched, they seemed to cloud over and the man slumped to the floor.

The man whose gun hand Remo was gripping pulled free. He tried to club down on Remo's skull with the heavy automatic. It was a simple reflex attack, to lash out with the closest weapon at hand, and Remo's response was equally reflex. Without thinking, he pushed his right hand up deep under the man's sternum, until he felt ribs and organs crack and crush, and the man fell to the floor dead.

Both dead. Remo stood up and looked at both of them in disgust.

"I hope you're satisfied now," he told Chiun.

"I am, I am," said Chiun. "I never saw this before. Did you know the baggage for people on the plane comes down a long chute and then goes around and around in a circle on a special carrier? Look, Remo, this is really interesting." He was standing on tiptoe, craning to get a better look at the baggage return, pointing below, and signaling for Remo to come look.

Remo ignored him. He quickly frisked the men's pockets and found the identification he had been looking for.

"Look at this, Remo," Chiun called again. "This is really good. The bags come down and then go all around and people take them off and if they miss, they come around again. Why is it that I have never seen this before?"

"Because you're too lazy to handle your own bags," Remo said.

"That is unkind," Chiun said. He turned back toward the window.

"Like that, huh?" Remo mumbled under his breath. "Like watching the baggage carousel, huh? Watch this."

He lifted the two bodies under his arms and pushed through a connecting door into the cargo staging area, where he tossed the two men onto a conveyor belt. A moment later, eyes wide open in death, their bodies contorted in the throes of their last moments, the two mustachioed men pitched headfirst down the baggage chute and hit the carousel. The bodies piled up for a moment in a lump, and then one at a time began rotating around the baggage pickup area. Women screamed. Children ran forward to get a closer look. Men looked at each other, puzzled, then looked around for a policeman.

Back inside the cargo office, Chiun watched, then turned from the window and glared at Remo when he reentered.

"Really, Remo. You find a way to cheapen everything," he said.

"Come on," Remo said. "We've got places to go."

When Mustafa Kaffir had turned out the light in his room at the Libyan mission, he had looked out the window into the street, as he always did, to make sure the New York City police guard was there, as it always was.

A half-hour later there was a faint tapping on his door, and then the door swung open, and in the brief light from the hallway, he saw the thin girlish figure of his personal assistant, who came across the carpeted floor noiselessly, peeled off his long robe, and slid into bed beside Kaffir.

They were asleep in each other's arms in minutes, and they slept soundly, until an hour later when Kaffir was awakened by one hand touching his shoulder, and prevented from crying out by another hand clapped over his mouth.

In the dim moonlight through the window, he recognized the hard face of the young American who had been to the mission to talk to him about

Bobby Jack Billings. Standing behind the American at the door was another figure. Kaffir could not see clearly in the dimness but it was a small person in a long robe, and then some reflected auto lights bounced into the room, and he saw the man by the door was an aged Oriental.

The American was whispering in his ear now.

"I think we should just let your little friend sleep," he told Kaffir. "But if that's what you want, this time you cooperate. You understand?"

Kaffir was slow in responding and he felt a bite of pain in his shoulder, a stab that felt inflicted by a knife, but as quickly as it came, it passed, and he nodded his head vigorously.

"The girl, the big blonde, when I asked you about her, you said you didn't know her," Remo said.

Kaffir shook his head. "You asked if she had come to question me," he said. "She hadn't."

"Don't split hairs," Remo said. "Where is she now?"

"She has gone to Boston.'

"Why?"

Kaffir hesitated. He felt the bite of pain again in his shoulder. Quickly, he said, "You know her mission?"

"Tell me," Remo said.

"She looks for that missing person."

"For Bobby Jack?" Remo said.

Kaffir nodded in the dark. Next to him, his young lover stirred, and he whispered at Remo, "She said she had a lead in Boston."

"What lead?" asked Remo.

"She didn't say. She called earlier and said she

would be going to Boston. She asked for two men to protect her on her way to the airport."

"Yeah," Remo said. "We met them."

"Oh?" said Kaffir.

"Yeah. Don't hold supper for them. She didn't say where she was going in Boston or who she was going to see?"

"No," Kaffir said. "She didn't. I swear it."

"Is she working for you?" Remo asked.

"Yes. That is, for my country."

"Why do you want to find Bobby Jack so much?" asked Remo.

"It was our hope that if we find him and return him safe to his brother-in-law, he might show his appreciation in tangible ways," Kaffir said.

Remo nodded. "If you're lying to me . . ." he said. "Well, I just hope you're not lying to me."

"I'm not," Kaffir said. "I'm not." He heard the reassuring deep breathing of his lover next to him. It gave him a sense of confidence and power. "I am telling the truth," he said.

"If you're not," said Remo, "I'll be back."

And then, as quickly and quietly as he had appeared ,the American was gone, and so was the old Oriental who had stood by the door. Involuntarily, Kaffir's hand reached for the telephone. He should tell someone. Who? The security guard. His superiors. Someone. He let his hand settle down slowly on the telephone.

Why bother, he thought. So far, the American, whoever he was, had learned very little. If the American government had known more, Washington would have been burning up the Libyan mission with visitors and protests. This American and his Oriental companion might be nothing more than freelancers, and they might very well meet fatal accidents in the normal course of their freelance duties. He took his hand from the telephone. There was nothing to be gained by saying anything to anyone. Not just now. He began to roll over in the bed, and then paused. Perhaps he should notify Jessica Lester. Warn her? He shook his head to himself in the dark. There was no need for that. She could take care of herself.

He wrapped his brawny arms around his lover who purred warmly, and Mustafa Kaffir closed his eyes and went to sleep.

CHAPTER TEN

Aboard the DC-9 to Boston, Remo explained his theory of the case to Chiun, who was following his usual procedure of staring at the wing to make sure it stayed on.

"Jessica kidnapped Bobby Jack," Remo said. "And she's got him stashed somewhere up in Boston. The Libyan, he was telling the truth. Probably, she's trying to sell them Bobby Jack." Remo was annoyed at Chiun's lack of response. "Anyway, that's the way I've got it figured."

Chiun slowly turned from the window. Below them, the sparse bright lights of the metropolitan area dimmed in the distance.

"Did I ever tell you," Chiun asked, "how the great master Tang-Si made soup with a nail?"

"No," said Remo, "and I don't think I want to hear about it."

"It was many of your centuries ago," Chiun said. "Tang-Si was one of the first great masters, even though he was not as great as the great Wang, but he was quite good. On an overall scale, I would place him—"

"C'mon, Little Father," said Remo. "If you're going to do it anyway, can't you get on with it?"

"This was one of the periods of time when the village of Sinanju faced starvation. Times were hard and the people were poor. Tang-Si was gone from the village for many months, and the poor people were on the verge of starvation. Even worse, they were ready to send the children home to the sea."

Remo groaned softly. "I know, Chiun, I know. Very poor . . . bad times . . . nothing to feed kids . . . villagers throw them in the North Korea Sea . . . call it sending the children home to the sea . . . I know all about it."

"You are very graceless," Chiun said. "But when the master Tang-Si came back from his journey, the people were desperate and they said, 'You must feed us, Master, even if it takes a miracle.' And the master, who had looked around the village and seen that the fishing nets were torn and that the sparse land had no seed in it, was angry, but he did not show it. Instead, he said, 'If you would see a miracle, I will show you how to make soup with a nail.'

"And he heated a large metal pot of water, and into it he threw an iron nail. When the water boiled, the villagers looked into the pot, but they saw no soup; they saw only water with a nail in the bottom of the pot.

"Then the great Tang-Si reached into his bag and pulled out carrots which he threw into the pot, and a special green radish which we grew, and chestnuts, and pieces of a rabbit he had caught, and soon a delicious soup was bubbling over the fire. And that, the great master told them, is how you make soup with a nail. A lot of water, a nail, a few

115

carrots, a special green radish, chestnuts and rabbit."

Chiun stopped talking and turned back to the window.

Remo tapped him on the shoulder.

"I don't get it," he said. "That's not making soup with a nail."

Chiun shook his head as he turned back. "What the master was saying to the villagers was that it was one thing to wish for miracles, but it would have been better in his absence, if they had fixed their nets and fished, and if they had sown seed in their fields. This is what the great master Tang-Si was telling our people."

He turned back to the window.

Remo thought about the story almost to Boston, then tapped Chiun on the shoulder again. The old man, satisfied that the wing seemed committed to its present position, turned to him again.

"This has got to mean something," Remo said. "What are you telling me about this case?"

"That you are trying to make soup with a nail. And in your case, you do not have carrots, the special green radishes we like, chestnuts or pieces of rabbit. You have nothing but the nail of a foolish idea."

Remo folded his arms stubbornly. "I think it's just the way I said it is." He looked hard toward the front of the plane. The stewardess caught him glaring at her and turned away in fright.

"You may think that," Chiun said. "That does not make it true."

"You're just angry about the Olympics," Remo said. "That's why you keep coming down on me."

"No," Chiun said. "I have resolved that promblem."

"Yeah?"

"Yes. Since I cannot bring myself to wear little shorts and shirts in the run for the Gold, you will do it for me since you do not mind looking ridiculous."

"Me?" said Remo.

"Yes. You will go and run around and jump and win a lot of medals, and then I will be your manager when you come home and I will make you rich beyond your wildest dreams."

"If I say yes, you will stop being nasty to me?"

"There is that possibility," Chiun said.

"I'll think about it," Remo said. "If I did it, I'd want a ninety-ten split on all money we made."

Chiun shook his head. "Do you think I am grasping?" he said. "I could not do that to you, Remo. You can keep fifteen percent."

"Me? Fifteen percent?"

"All right. Ten percent," Chiun said. "Let's not bicker. It is unseemly."

"Little Father," Remo said.

"Yes, my son?"

"Go make soup with a nail."

Although it was well after midnight, Remo called Smith from Logan Airport in Boston.

Casting a knowing eye at Chiun, he told Smith his theory that the blonde woman had kidnapped Bobby Jack Billings.

"Remo, that's ridiculous," Smith said.

"Yeah? Well, if you and Chiun are so smart, you tell me what's going down."

"The woman's name is Jessica Lester?" Smith asked.

"I think so."

"All right," Smith said. "Try this. Jessica Lester is looking for Billings, just as you are. She traced him to PLOTZ, and then she found out something that's sending her to Boston."

"And what about the Libyans?" Remo asked.

"They were the first ones to know that Billings was gone," Smith said. "Maybe Washington's cover story that he was off on a drunken tear didn't fool them. Wait just a moment."

Remo could hear Smith fumbling with some paper on his desk.

"Here it is, Remo," Smith said. "Jessica Lester. Age 32. British passport. South African national. Worked for MI-5 for seven years. Exceptional skills as a field agent. Outstanding marksman, hand-to-hand combat. Resigned four years ago. Reported to be working privately for governments of various countries." Smith stopped reading. "That's it. She was probably hired by the Libyans to run down Billings."

"Well, maybe," Remo said grudgingly.

"It makes more sense than your idea," Smith said.

"Smitty," Remo said.

"Yes?"

"Go make soup with a nail."

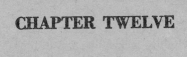

CHAPTER TWELVE

Jessica Lester straightened the shoulder straps of her white nylon nightgown, pulled down the covers of her bed and, as she did every night, transferred a small .25 caliber pistol from her overnight bag to a spot under her pillow.

Tomorrow. Tomorrow, she was sure, she would run down Bobby Jack Billings. And then? And then she didn't care. Her job would be finished.

Like a child with an unworried mind, she fell asleep almost as soon as her head touched the pillow, sleeping on her back in the queenly unprotected position that indicates faith in and contentment with the world.

She did not know how long she slept before she felt a hand touch her left shoulder and a voice whisper in her ear, "All right, Jessica, where is he?"

She pulled away from the hand as she sat bolt upright in the bed. She turned her eyes to her left. In the dim moonlight that sifted in through her twentieth-floor windows, she saw the face of Remo, the man she had met at PLOTZ headquarters, the man she had suspected as dangerous and had left orders to intercept.

He was lying in her bed, looking at her. She turned her body around to face him, so her left hand rested on the mattress near her pillow. She sneaked her fingers in under the pillow until she could feel the cold metal of the pistol. It gave her a sense of reassurance.

"What are you doing here?" She looked toward the door. The portable lock she always carried in her bag was still in place. So was the chair which was jammed under the doorknob.

"Looking for Bobby Jack Billings," Remo said.

"How'd you get in here?" she asked.

"I'd tell you the truth that I walked up the outside wall, but you wouldn't believe it anyway, so why not just let it slide. Let's stay with my question. Where is he?"

"Who is Bobby whatever-his-name-is?" she asked.

"Sorry, honey, that won't wash. It's Bobby Jack, he's the president's brother-in-law, and I've been looking for him just like you've been. So where is he?"

"Who are you working for?" she asked.

"The government," Remo answered casually, "and I've been one step behind you ever since I started."

"I don't know what you mean but you've got a lot of nerve barging in here and—"

"I didn't barge. I climbed."

"Coming in here and crawling into my bed. I've got a good mind to call the manager."

"Why not?" Remo said. "While you're at it, call

the FBI so we can have you hauled off for spying."

Her left hand was now comfortably curled around the grip of the revolver and the feeling of the cold metal in the palm of her hand gave her a renewed sense of confidence. It wouldn't hurt, she realized, to talk to this Remo and find out what he knew. If he alone knew about her, that was one thing; but if there were a massive number of U.S. agents on her trail, that might require rethinking her position.

"I don't usually conduct interviews in my bed," she said.

"Break a rule just this once," Remo said. He stretched out his right hand and touched her neck just under the jawline. Her flesh tingled where he touched it and she pulled her head back away from him.

"No hands," she said.

"Whatever you like," Remo said. He pulled his hand away and folded both his arms across his stomach. He was unarmed, Jessica saw.

She lay back down on her pillow, moving her gun hand under Remo's pillow. Her pistol barrel was now only several inches from his skull. An error and he was a dead man.

"How much do you know about me?" she asked.

"Enough," Remo said. "Your name's Jessica Lester and you used to be with British Secret Service before you went private. You're working for the Libyans. You're looking for Bobby Jack but I don't really know why. Why?"

"How'd you know I was working for the Libyans?" she asked.

"I should have known right away because you

didn't interview them like you did the Secret Service men. That should have been a tip, but it didn't register. If you hadn't spoken to them, it had to mean that you had already gotten all the information they had and that could only come if you were working for them."

"I should have remembered to tell them to say I had interviewed them," she said.

She saw Remo shake his head in the darkened room. "It wouldn't have mattered. I would have known if they lied to me. Anyway, I went back there tonight and they 'fessed up that you were one of theirs. What are they paying you?"

"A hundred thousand dollars if I find Bobby Jack before you people do. Another hundred thousand if I can deliver him to them."

"Why the hell would anybody want him?" Remo asked.

"I don't know. I didn't ask, but I guess that they figure if they have him, they can use him to get some concessions from the president. I know they're trying to buy plutonium."

"Could be," Remo said. "You know, you're very good."

"Thank you. I think I am."

"You fooled me when I met you at PLOTZ," Remo said. "The bandanna around your head broke the train of my thought. I was looking for a tall blonde with long braided hair and you didn't register."

"That's what I figured. I wasn't taking any chances." She noticed that Remo's right hand had moved out now and was touching her knee. It felt good and she no longer felt threatened because she had the gun under his pillow. He touched the inside of her left knee and she fought an impulse to squirm.

"How'd you find out about PLOTZ?" he asked. "How'd you learn about the note from Bobby Jack?"

"The president must have mentioned it to his press secretary. And the secretary was in a cocktail lounge that night, drinking more than was good for him, and he happened to mention it to a person I know who passed it along to me."

"That simple?"

"This kind of work usually is," Jessica said. Remo did not agree. He found the work unbearably complicated and hard but he did not want to let her know that.

The feeling along her left leg was pleasure and pain commingled, the feeling of a limb that had fallen asleep and was now tingling back to life, a sensation of total awareness of that part of her body. Jessica Lester had already made up her mind to kill him but there was no point in hurrying, she decided. If he had something else on his mind, his death could be postponed for a few moments.

"It wasn't just any woman in any cocktail lounge," Jessica said. "The woman works for me. She makes it a habit to stay close to everybody in Washington who's got a big mouth and who drinks too much."

"I see," Remo said.

"And who are you?" Jessica asked.

"Not yet," Remo said. "So where'd it lead after PLOTZ?"

She stretched her leg slightly as if to encourage

128

Remo's hand to move more along the length of her leg. Remo lay back and changed from his left hand to his right hand.

"I pilfered the files while you were out with that dip Zentz," she said. "I found out the money source was Earl Slimone and so I came up here to go to his headquarters."

"Earl who?" Remo asked.

"Earl Slimone. He's a banker. I was going to see him in the morning."

"What's he got to do with anything?"

"I don't know. I know he put up the money for PLOTZ. And he gave them word that they should be as public as they could be. What happened to that Zentz, by the way?"

"He died in a fire."

"Too bad."

"Yes, wasn't it?" Remo's hand was now on her upper thigh.

"So what do you want from me?" she asked.

"What do you think?" Remo said.

Jessica rolled over and onto Remo. She pressed her body tight to his. Her hands, between them, busied themselves with his clothing, and then there was a magical, moist time during which Jessica momentarily lost hold of the pistol under the pillow and Remo said, "What I want is for you to leave town."

Jessica rolled back to her side of the bed. The French called orgasm "le petit mort"—the little death—and she lay limply for a moment in the throes of the little death, and then remembered another kind of death. The large death.

129

She closed her hand around the pistol, and brought the weapon out from under Remo's pillow.

"I'm sorry," she said.

"Are you?" Remo asked. He lifted his body up on his arms to look into her face. "Sorry for what?"

"For having to kill you."

"Oh, that," Remo said.

She put the muzzle of the gun to Remo's temple. "Goodbye," she said.

"So long," Remo replied.

She squeezed the trigger. The click was loud and metallic in the silent bedroom, but there was no explosion. Frantically, she squeezed the trigger again. Another click.

"Don't bother," Remo said. "Do you think I'd leave a gun with bullets in it under your pillow?"

Anger surged in Jessica.

"There's more than one way to use a gun," she hissed. She pulled her gun hand away from Remo's temple, then swung the pistol back to smash it into his skull.

"And more than one way to protect against it," Remo said. She felt his hand close over the gun which stopped as if she had slammed it against a wall. She felt the pistol removed from her hand. She felt cold metal drop onto her bare stomach: one piece, then another. She looked down and saw the gun broken into pieces.

Remo hopped up out of bed. "Well," he said airily, "if I spend any more time here, I'm going to be late for the rest of my calls."

He walked toward the window that looked out over Copley Square. He opened the window high and then turned to her again.

130

"Jessica," he said, "I'm serious. You're done with this case. Pack up and leave. The next time, I might have to do something I don't want to do."

"All right," she said. "I understand." She realized that Remo was serious about going out the window, and she looked again at the two halves of the gun on her stomach and suddenly believed that he could do it.

"I've got one question," she said.

"Shoot."

"Why'd you come in through the window instead of the door?"

"My manager," Remo said. "He wants me to start getting in shape for the Olympics."

Before she could ask another question, Remo had jumped feet first through the open window. She expected to hear the scream of a falling man, but there was no scream, only silence. And something prevented her from going to the window to look out.

Instead, she got up out of the bed quickly, turned on a light and began to toss her few clothes into her overnight bag. She had given up the name of Earl Slimone, but she was still far ahead of Remo. She could clean the assignment up and be gone, before he ever caught up to her again.

She stopped for a moment in the middle of her packing. There was something else she could do that would buy time too.

She looked up a number in the Boston telephone directory and dialed it.

"Hello, is this Mr. Slimone's home? You don't know me, but I just want you to know that someone is planning to attack Mr. Slimone tonight at his home."

She paused and listened.

"That's right," she said. "His home in Boston. The man will be there soon. His name is Remo."

CHAPTER THIRTEEN

Remo called Smith from an outside phone booth in Copley Square.

"Have you found the woman?" Smith asked.

"Yes," Remo said. "Don't worry about her. Who is Earl Slimone?"

There was a pause on the other end of the line. "What about Earl Slimone?" Smith asked.

"That's who she was on her way up here to see," Remo said.

Chiun appeared outside the booth. He motioned to Remo that he should jog up and down while talking to Smith. Remo shook his head. Chiun jogged up and down in place, to demonstrate.

"I'm damned if I'm going to be hopping up and down in a telephone booth," Remo said. Chiun shrugged. Smith said, "Who asked you to hop up and down in a phone booth?"

"Forget it," Remo said. "What about Slimone?"

"That complicates everything," Smith said. "Slimone is a banker with mob connections. A federal grand jury was getting ready to investigate his role

in financing the last presidential campaign. And
. . . oh, no."

"What?" Remo asked.

"Another grand jury was looking into Billings
and what he might have had to do with financing
his brother-in-law's campaign."

"Then there's our connection," Remo said.

"It's worse than that," Smith said.

"Why?"

"Suppose that Billings was the conduit for mob
money into the presidential campaign. And now
Billings turns up missing. You see what it might
mean?"

"No," Remo said.

"It might be the thing we feared. Maybe the
president himself is behind the disappearance.
Maybe Slimone didn't just kidnap Billings so he
wouldn't talk—maybe the president ordered the
kidnapping."

"Well, you worry about things like that," Remo
said. "All I want to do is track the guy down.
Where's Slimone's place up here?"

He waited while Smith consulted CURE's com-
puters, and then the agency head was back on the
telephone with an address in the Back Bay section
of Boston.

"Thanks, Smitty. I'll keep you posted."

Remo hung up and stepped outside the booth.
Chiun said, "You will never amount to anything if
you do not practice."

"Can it, Chiun. I've got other things on my
mind."

"This Bobby Jobby Billings?" Chiun asked.

"Bobby Jack. Yeah."

"Does he pay us our wages? Does he pay the small tribute that goes to my village?"

"No."

"Then who cares about him?" Chiun asked. "Really, Remo, you have to talk to Smith about the assignments he gives you. Using you to gallivant around the countryside looking for some noisy fat person is like using a surgeon's scalpel to cut firewood."

"A job's a job," Remo said. "It keeps me busy."

"And so does cutting firewood keep a scalpel busy. But when you need the scalpel for surgery, it does not perform well anymore."

"Are you saying I could be losing my edge?"

"You might be," Chiun said. "Now if you were to undergo a vigorous program of training and exercise, I could probably keep you in some kind of reasonable condition. It would be an effort, but I might be able to."

"Forget it."

"You could start with running in place," Chiun said.

"Never."

"Think about running in place," Chiun said.

"Where is his apartment?" Chiun asked as they stood across the street from the fourteen-story apartment building that housed Earl Slimone.

"Top floor, of course," Remo said.

"Of course," Chiun said. It was an oddity, he thought, that people believed that height gave them security. "We should go in through the top."

"I've been up and down a building already tonight," Remo said. "You're not going to wear down my tired body just so you can get your hands on my gold medals. We'll go in the front door."

Inside the front door, they were met by a doorman. Remo noticed that he had a scar over his right eye and that he needed a shave.

"Can I help youse guys?" he said.

"Yes. We're calling on Earl Slimone," Remo said.

"At this hour?" the doorman said. He rubbed his bristly face with his hand.

"Well, obviously at this hour," Remo said. "Who do you think you're talking to? The ghosts of Christmas Past?"

"They expecting you?"

CHAPTER FOURTEEN

"No, but I'm sure you'll straighten all that out," Remo said.

The doorman seemed to think for a moment.

"All right. You can go up. Use the center elevator." He pointed to a bank of elevators twenty feet down the hall.

Remo pressed the up button. The right elevator door opened. He and Chiun started to step inside but were halted by a shout from the doorman.

"I said use the middle one. That one don't go all the way upstairs."

"Okay," Remo said. He and Chiun waited, with the doorman standing behind them, for a full minute before the center elevator arrived.

The door opened and the doorman pushed them from behind. They allowed themselves to stumble into the elevator where they were faced by two more men, needing shaves but not needing guns. Each man carried a heavy .45 automatic in his hand.

"You Remo?" one of them asked.

"That's right."

"Good. We been waiting for you."

Remo was surprised. Then he realized. Jessica Lester had blown the whistle on them. That was one he owed her.

"You going to kill us here?" Remo asked.

"No. We gonna talk to you upstairs and *then* kill you," one of the men said.

"Is Slimone here?" Remo asked.

"Naah, he ain't here."

"Where is he?"

"Hey, you ain't asking no questions around here. You're gonna be answering questions. You just don't come in here and start asking questions like that."

"Do you know where he is?" Remo said.

"No. Nobody tells us nothing."

"Then we don't need you," Remo said. The elevator had risen smoothly and quietly. It was slowing now as it reached the fourteenth floor penthouse. Without turning, Remo waved his hand behind him and the two automatics were knocked from the men's hands and dropped onto the carpeted elevator floor. As the men scrambled down to pick them up, the elevator door opened. Chiun stepped outside and Remo hit the down button. He stepped out quickly. The two men had their guns in their hands again and were raising them toward Remo. He kicked into the elevator with his right foot. Tap, tap. The guns were knocked loose again. Remo stepped outside and the elevator door closed behind him. The elevator started down.

He and Chiun waited a moment for the elevator to clear the floor. Using his fingers as chisels, Remo drove his hands into the opening between the two doors. He pulled the doors apart and held them open.

Chiun moved in alongside Remo and flashed out his left foot at the inch-thick steel cable on which the elevator rode. The cable shuddered, then threaded and snapped. Remo looked down at the roof of the elevator car as it began to plunge down the shaft. He heard the shouts of the men. He took his hands from the door and let them close quietly behind him.

A few seconds later, there was a loud thump

140

down below, in the elevator shaft. The screams suddenly stopped, and all was silence.

"All right," Remo said. "Let's find out where Slimone is."

They were in an anteroom that faced two doors. The center door was unlocked and they stepped into a large posh leather and wood living room.

A young man sat on a sofa. He looked up at the door expectantly. His face clouded over when he saw Remo and Chiun enter, alone. The young man dove for a small table. His hand fished inside the drawer before Remo kicked the drawer shut, with the man's hand inside. He held the drawer closed with his foot.

"We ask once," Remo said. "Where is he?"

"His estate. Newport, Rhode Island."

"How long's he been there?"

"Almost a week. He's resting."

"Who's there with him?"

"Nobody."

Remo pressed harder on the drawer.

"Honest. Just usual security people is all."

"Thank you," Remo said.

He released the pressure of his foot on the drawer. The man came out with a gun, aimed at Remo. Before he could squeeze the trigger, Remo's heel was planted under his jaw, lifting, the pressure increasing, until the man's skull separated from his spinal column.

"And thanks again," Remo said as the man fell into a heap. He looked at Chiun and shrugged. "I was wondering what I was going to do with him so he didn't call Newport."

141

Chiun looked at the body. "You seem to have found a solution," he said.

At the airport, Remo went into the private pilot's lounge and found a pilot who would fly them immediately to Newport for four hundred dollars. As they were walking to the twin-engined Cessna, the pilot said, "Too bad."

"What's too bad?" Remo asked.

"If you were an hour earlier, you could've shared the ride. I had another passenger."

"Blonde? Tall, good looking?" Remo asked.

"That's her. Said she was running away from her husband. Hey, you're not her husband, are you?"

"Would it matter?"

"Not if you pay me in advance,' the pilot said.

CHAPTER FIFTEEN

Two hundred thousand dollars.

The amount reverberated through Jessica Lester's mind all through the short flight from Boston to Newport. And she kept mouthing the words to herself when she locked herself into a toilet booth in the small private airport and began to change her clothes.

Two hundred thousand dollars.

In the bottom of her small overnight bag she found a black shirt, black slacks and black walking shoes.

As she dressed, she thought that Remo had told her very little but he had told her enough. He was from the United States government and was going to try to get back Bobby Jack Billings. In simplest terms, that meant Remo was trying to steal two hundred thousand dollars from her, the amount she had been promised by the Libyans if she could produce Bobby Jack for them.

"No way," she said aloud. Two hundred thousand dollars added to her already substantial bank ac-

144

counts in Europe and Jessica could neatly retire from the business.

It had been many years since she had first come from South Africa to become a field agent in Britain's MI-5. It had quickly become apparent to her that there was no room for a woman to move up in the British system, to take a position of prominence, no matter how much she might have deserved it. There was just too much male domination, too many old school ties, too much reliance on how many hyphens you had in your name, to permit a young and beautiful South African to reach her level. The Peter Principle, she had once observed to a friend, seemed to work only for those who had peters.

She bided her time. She often requested transfers so she could get field duty in as much of Europe as possible, where she went out of her way to meet as many agents of other governments as she could. Then one day, after five years in the field, she typed out a neat resignation and dropped it on the desk of her station chief. That same day, she let all her acquaintances from other governments know that she was available for contract jobs.

They were not long in coming. Things had to be delivered, people had to be contacted, items had to be stolen—and the jobs were always risky enough that the government which wanted them done could not risk assigning one of their own agents, lest he be caught and the country embarrassed or worse. Jessica could do the jobs and, if she were caught, quite honestly say that she did not know for whom she was working, since most of her assignments came through an interlock of agents, with the actual assignment being outlined to her by an agent she had never met before, an agent who was just doing a favor for another agent of another government and who might someday ask for just the same kind of a favor in return. Even with her identity exposed, the capturing government could do no more than rail that she was a British agent, and in her mind that would be what Great Britain deserved for driving her out into private enterprise.

The jobs and the money rolled in. Jessica Lester was a well-trained agent, as were most British spies since, with the possible exception of the Israelis, the British ran the best cloak and dagger operation in the world.

She had been at it now for three years, working both sides against the middle, the middle against both ends, and she knew it was time to get out because lately she had begun to be nervous on missions. She had been told about that in her earliest days of spy training. Her instructor, a whiskered old man with rheumy blue eyes, had said that there would come a time when she would feel she wanted to quit the business. When it happened, he said, that was the time to quit because there was a subtle psychological change in the agent that made him less sure of himself, less willing to take a chance, and in the process, made him less likely to survive.

"It's really a function of the back of the head, girl," he had said. "Of your subconscious mind. One day, it just totes up all the columns and says you've stayed too long, best take your leave. When it happens, take your leave before it's too late."

"What happens if you don't?" she had asked.

"Two things can happen. You can get caught or you can get killed, and in this business, they're often the same thing, don't you know. And if you're lucky enough not to be caught or killed, you wind up doing what I'm doing—training other fools to go into the field."

"Did it happen to you?" she asked.

"The second day I was on the job," he said with a chuckle. "Fortunately, my uncle was in the ministry and I was able to get assigned to training duty immediately. Thank heavens. I would have been a terrible field hand. And besides I hate dying."

She had been inclined to dismiss it as the rambling of an old cowardly incompetent and had put it farther and farther out of her mind, until one evening, she was standing on a street corner in Copenhagen, waiting for someone to deliver a package to her, when the question hit her sharply: "What am I doing here? For God's sake, I might be killed."

At that moment, she remembered the old instructor's words and she did a quick recap of her life. She was almost 32 years old. She was beautiful and intelligent and she had a substantial amount of money in the bank.

But not quite enough. Not quite enough to retire the way she wanted to retire. She kept taking private missions, but she knew her career, to all intents and purposes, was over. And then the Libyans sought her out and told her about the disappearance of Bobby Jack Billings and that they would pay two hundred thousand dollars to get their hands on him, so she took the job. It met all the qualifications. It was the one large score she needed to have enough to retire on her own terms. The chances for danger were slight, and, best of all, if she were captured it would be by the United States which made it a practice, almost unique in the world, of not killing spies found working inside its borders.

She finished dressing and thought of Remo and her groin tingled. She wondered if he might be near the point of resigning himself, and then she thought sadly of the reception she had arranged for him back at Earl Slimone's Boston apartment and she put him out of her head. He was dead by now. Dead, because he had the look and feel of a zealot, a patriot, who could be deflected only by bullets from what he considered his mission in life.

She pulled up the leg of her black jeans and strapped a leather holster to the inside of her calf. Into it, she put a small .22 caliber pistol. In another holster, hung from her belt at the small of her back, she hung a .32 caliber snub-nosed revolver.

She took a black kerchief from the bottom of her overnight bag and stuffed it into the pocket of her trench coat. The trench coat was oyster white and she wore it to eliminate the possible notion in people's mind that they had seen a six-foot-tall woman dressed all in black. The trench coat changed that vision of her and when she got to her job, she would simply take off the coat and leave it by the side of the road.

She would never need it again.

After they arrived at the Newport airfield, Remo told Chiun: "I think we've got the beat on her.

148

She'll probably wait till daylight to case the Slimone place."

Chiun shook his head. "Every path is a highway for one whose feet are sure."

"Which means?"

"It means that this is an intelligent and talented woman. I am sure she can work at night. After all, I taught you to work at night, picked it of many possible things to try to teach you, because even cats learn it quickly and you are at least as smart as a cat, they being the most stupid creatures in God's universe."

"All right, we'll go now. But it's not like you to want to hurry," Remo said.

"Who knows?" Chiun said. "If we are successful, we shall earn the president's everlasting gratitude. Who knows what good things that might provide in the future?"

"Like naming me to the Olympic team?" Remo said.

"You really are a most distrusting person," Chiun said.

It was 4:15 A.M.

CHAPTER SIXTEEN

It was called The Springs and it had once been a summer retreat for the entire Lippincott family, which was to money in America what the Ford family was to automobiles.

But somewhere along the line, the practice of entire families all vacationing together in what was basically a large compound had gone out of style and finally even the Lippincotts had surrendered to economic reality and sold the unused place with its main mansion and its dozen smaller buildings on the edge of the ocean in Newport.

The next owner had decided to make a resort of the place. Anticipating a swarm of rich guests, he had run an electric rail spur into the compound. He had carved up the main house into a luxury hotel and the smaller buildings into apartments for family groups. On the rolling grounds, he had built a nine-hole golf course. He put in new docks with pleasure boats offering sightseeing cruises, and a small air strip for private planes.

He had everything except guests. The Springs was too high-priced for New Englanders and not far enough away for New Yorkers whose vacation tastes began to run more and more to Florida.

The owner had held it as long as he could. Just when he was fearful that he might have to declare bankruptcy and drop the whole idea, World War II began and he was able to sell The Springs to the federal government, which wanted the secluded estate as a training base for spies going overseas.

After the war, the United States kept the property as a rehabilitation and rest center for returning staff officers suffering from fatigue. What this actually meant was that it was a hospital for generals who had gotten a dose of overseas clap.

After that the property languished. For a time, there was a possibility of its being developed as a presidential retreat, but during the war President Roosevelt had favored Shangri-La and President Eisenhower had expanded that area and rechristened it as Camp David and so the old Lippincott estate was left to lie fallow, until one day a Congressional budget committee found it on the books and ordered it sold at auction.

It was exactly what Earl Slimone had wanted and he gladly played the $2.4 million price tag. Slimone had gotten rich in the black market during World War II, selling counterfeit ration coupons for gas and meat.

He had vision. He foresaw that while the war had been a good time for making money, it would be nothing compared to the post-war period. He saw the United States making moves around the world to bolster up allies, to create alliances, to strengthen its position, and he saw no reason why organized crime could not do the same thing. Soon

The Springs became the meeting place for shadowy people from France, Italy, Scandinavia, and the Far East.

Here were made the agreements that divided the world into crime zones. The time zones of the world began at the Greenwich Meridian in England, but the crime zones began in Newport, Rhode Island.

Slimone's empire blossomed and as it did and as he grew older, Slimone began to think more and more about garnering public respect. He collected committee chairmanships as some men collected stamps or honorary degrees or women. He became the founder of this, the benefactor of that, the sponsor of something else. Seven universities in the United States had chairs of philosophy endowed by him, although the only philosophy Earl Slimone had ever devised was an improvement on the American mercantile idea of "buy cheap and sell dear." Slimone's philosophy had improved it to "steal for free and make them pay their lungs to buy it."

In the fifties, Slimone began to tinker in political campaigns when he saw a growing tendency in the government to look into the people and the businesses of organized crime. He guaranteed himself that he would be on the winning side by supporting both sides. And as crime in the world became a more stable instrument, which required fewer summit meetings and in which the lines of communication and supply were increasingly simple, the old estate slowly became Slimone's main home where he entertained the rich and the powerful from around the world. And when he took them to play golf on his private nine-hole course, he sometimes had to remind himself not to laugh when he realized that this foreign minister or that ambassador were putting on greens that were unusually lush and rich because they were fertilized by unusually lush and rich organic waste—the bodies of people who had disagreed with Slimone and quite simply disappeared to become forever a part of the Rhode Island landscape.

In the late moonlight, Remo could see the twelve-foot-high electrified fence surrounding the estate. Around the top of the fence was particularly brutish-looking barbed wire, chosen personally by Slimone because each wrap had six barbs instead of the usual four.

"It's a big place," Remo said as he looked through the fence toward the ocean behind. The silhouettes of half a dozen buildings loomed in front of them. "He could be anywhere."

"The big house," Chiun said. "Up and over."

Remo looked at the high fence, the height of two tall men. He grabbed Chiun about the waist and slung him upward to a tree. Chiun landed lightly on his feet on the first limb, then ran along it toward the fence. When he ran out of tree, he dove through the air, over the fence, landing lightly on his feet on the grass on the other side of the chain mesh.

He looked back at Remo.

"Why are you waiting there?" he hissed.

Remo leaped up to the tree branch, catching it with his fingertips. He swung himself up onto the limb, and then followed Chiun's route to the end of the limb, diving over onto the lush grass just inside the fence. For good measure, he did a double somersault before landing. When he stopped on his feet, he threw his arms out to his sides at shoulder height.

"Always playing games," Chiun said.

"Just practicing for the Olympics," Remo said. "Anyway, nothing wrong with showing a little class."

"Economy is everything" Chiun said. "If one turn is needed, do one turn. Anything more is for show, mere show."

"You're just jealous."

"As the sun envies the candle," Chiun replied. "This way."

Jessica Lester had parked her car and sat in the front seat while she blackened her face with water-soluble makeup. Ordinarily, the high fence would have given her a moment's worry. But she had asked the pilot who flew her into Newport to go low over the estate and she had seen the rail lines glinting in the moonlight. There had to be an opening in the fence for a railroad car to get through.

She followed the fence to the far western edge of the property where it turned north, then followed the fence for five hundred yards in that direction. She had left her white trench coat in her automobile, parking in the shrubs, back off the main road, out of sight. Her light blonde hair was wrapped now and hidden in her black bandanna.

In the deepest part of the night before the onset of dawn, she moved quickly and surely toward a spot in the fence fifty yards away where she saw the twin lines of railroad track glistening in the moonlight.

Closer up, she could see the gap in the fence. As she expected, there was a guard on duty in a small shack next to the fence opening.

She moved away from the fence, traveling a large semi-circle in the blackness, which finally brought her back to the fence behind the guard's shack. Cautiously, she peered in through a window.

The guard was sitting on a stool, dozing. She reached behind her for her pistol and moved to the front of the shack where the door was ajar. Then she changed her mind. If she killed him and he was required to make certain check-in calls, it might trigger an alarm and alert the camp. She did not need to kill him. She moved away from the shack, through the opening in the electrified fence and vanished quickly in some shrubbery which bordered the rail line. The guard being alive might make it more difficult for her to get out with Bobby Jack Billings in tow, she realized, but she would blow up that little bridge when she came to it.

Still she felt a tinge of nervousness. Thank God, she thought, that this is the last mission. When the nerves went, a spy had nothing left, except perhaps guile and intelligence and experience. But without nerve, those things counted for less than nothing. Nerve was the key—and she was nervous and didn't like the feeling.

She wished it were all over before she made a mistake.

In a small room in an underground chamber farther down the railroad track, two men sat looking at a panel on which Jessica Lester's mistake was clearly visible.

She had correctly figured that the weakness of the compound was the train entrance. But the designers of the security procedures at The Spring had realized that human guards had human failings, like falling asleep at night. They had installed a backup system of invisible electric eyes, beginning twenty feet from the guard's shack. The system was installed on bushes two feet off the ground so it would not be triggered accidentally by a rabbit or a raccoon. So when the red warning light flashed on in the control room, the two men who sat in the room drinking coffee and watching the instrument panel were instantly alert. They knew someone had broken into the camp.

The two men wore military type khaki uniforms, with holstered sidearms on their hips. One of the men pressed a button which flashed small warning signals in one of the buildings in which the security staff of the compound slept. The small beeping sound instantly woke one of the men, who slept in his clothes. He got up from his bed and shook awake four other men who quickly dressed, strapped on guns and ran from the building.

Back at the underground control center, another red light flashed as Jessica Lester triggered another electric eye.

"Headed this way," the man said.

"I wonder if he killed Cooley," the second man said.

"Serves him right if he's sleeping again. Where are those guards?"

"Don't worry. They're coming. I wonder who this guy is."

"Don't know," the second man said. He was

short, with a build like a top-loading washer. "There's some funny stuff going on up at the big house. The maids tell me they're not allowed into the west wing. The old man brings in food himself. Most of it comes out not even touched. But they keep shipping in two cases of beer a day."

He stopped speaking as a third light lit on the panel. The lights were arranged in concentric rings. The new light lit on the third inner ring.

"Definitely heading for the big house," the man said. "I guess it's time."

The two men went outside the guard's control room and met five other men. They spoke quietly.

"He's heading up toward the big house," the husky short man said. "We'll cut him off up there."

He opened a door that led down a dark flight of steps. The men ran down the steps, closing the door behind them. At the bottom of the steps was a tunnel cut under the ground to the main building. The tunnel was lightly illuminated by low-wattage bulbs but the men were able to see well enough to run at full speed.

The tunnel exited at ground level from a shedlike structure attached to the rear of the main mansion. Next to the shed was a private railroad car sitting on a siding directly behind the rear patio entrance to the mansion. The men took up predetermined posts around the building and waited.

Jessica Lester took her pistol from behind her waist. From her pocket, she took a silencer and screwed it onto the barrel. As she moved near the big house now, she could see the first fingers of lightness growing in the pre-dawn sky. She would

have to move quickly or the same costume that pro-
vided protection in darkness would make her stand
out like a beacon light.

She was surprised that there were no significant
signs of security. It made no sense to shelter a kidnap victim and have no security but a fence with a
hole in it. She put the thought out of her mind. So
the mission was a piece of cake. After all these
years, she deserved an easy one for her valediction.

Just a few minutes more, she hoped.

"There are electronic devices," Chiun said to
Remo as they moved swiftly toward the big house.
"Do you feel them?"

"No," Remo said. "But I figured there were
'cause we didn't see any guards."

"There are," said Chiun flatly. Remo did not
need to ask Chiun how he knew there were electronic sensors. Remo knew how Chiun knew. It required exerting a force around one's body so that
anything intruding on that force was registered by
direction and strength. Remo could do it most of
the time, but it took a conscious effort of will for
him. With Chiun, it was an instinctive and continu-
ous process.

They were only a hundred yards from the big
house.

Jessica paused at the edge of the trees leading to
the clearing on which the house sat. She looked
around carefully. She could see no lights and no
guards. To the rear of the house, to her left, was a
private railroad car. The twin steel track led away

from the house through the big encampment. Instinctively, she went toward the rear of the building. Entry would probably be simpler there. She stepped cautiously over the railroad tracks. She didn't understand third rails and electricity but she had come too far to blunder now.

She saw that that railroad car sat next to a large patio with glass doors that led into the rear of the building. She straightened up and ran toward the doors. Just as she reached the flagstone patio, she felt arms tackling her about the ankles. She tried to aim the gun at her tackler, but the pistol was snatched from her hand.

She felt herself tossed over, roughly, onto her back. When she looked up, two men stood over her. One had a handgun pointed at her. Five more men ran up behind them. They all wore khaki uniforms, and had their weapons out of their holsters.

The man nearest her reached down and ripped her bandanna roughly from her head. Her long blonde braids fell out in stark contrast to her blackened face.

"Well, well, well. What have we here?" he said. "It's a woman, I do believe." He placed the open palm of his hand on her chest. "Yes, indeed. A woman."

He grabbed her hair and yanked her head around as he knelt down alongside her. "Some answers to some questions," he said. "And fast."

"You're hurting me," Jessica said. Her mind was working quickly. She twisted her body as if in pain, trying to work up the pants on her left leg. She wanted to get the gun in her hand. She knew she stood no chance against seven armed men but with the pistol in her hand, the crowd might thin out and she might have a chance of escape.

In the meantime, she had to take what they gave until they tired of their sport and took her to their boss. These six men in military uniforms were not responsible for the kidnapping of Bobby Jack Billings. Uniforms carried out plans; they didn't devise them.

Her long braids were caught in the husky man's hand, and as he rose to his feet he yanked her up to a standing position. Her hand pulled away from the gun strapped to her leg.

"Who are you?" he asked.

"The Avon Lady. I like to get an early start."

He backhanded a slap across her face and pressed his right arm up behind her back.

"Last chance," he said. "Who are you?"

"She's with us," came Remo's voice.

CHAPTER SEVENTEEN

The seven uniformed guards turned toward the end of the flagstone patio as Remo and Chiun came around the corner of the house and moved toward them.

Jessica Lester's heart surged again as she saw them. She had been sure that Remo was dead; she had never felt happier to see anyone before.

The guard holding Jessica's arm said, "What the hell is this, a convention?"

"Just let her go," Remo said, "before I peel your eyeballs."

"Why, sure," the guard said. "It'll be my pleasure. I prefer working on men anyway."

He released Jessica's arm and then, with a looping swing of his right arm, tried to bury the butt of his heavy automatic between Remo's eyes.

He missed, although Remo had not seemed to move. His action triggered the other guards into movement. The quarters were too close to consider firing their weapons, so they leaped forward on Remo and Chiun, swinging their guns, pummeling with their fists, a surging pile of humanity that seemed to swell and throb with a life of its own.

Jessica, forgotten for the moment, watched only a split second of the battle, then turned, opened the large French doors at the end of the patio and ran into the house. She was close to mission's end, she thought. It was worth a try. Perhaps if the diversion lasted long enough, she could find Bobby Jack Billings and spirit him off before anybody thought of her.

Buried under a pile of bodies, Remo and Chiun remained motionless for a moment, giving the surging guards a chance to create their own uniform rhythm of movement. They absorbed the rhythm as their own and then, slowly at first, but increasingly faster, they began to move, at first in time with the movement, but then more and more in counterpoint to it. Remo flicked a weapon from a hand, and Chiun flicked a hand from a wrist. Moving in circular forms now against the straight line force of their attackers, they sliced through them as if they were working in a different dimension of time and space. One guard raised the butt of his weapon over his head and smashed it down toward Remo's skull. But Remo had been in his zone of power only for a fleeting instant and when the gun butt struck skull, it was the skull of one of the other guards who dropped to the flagstone without a sound.

Remo circled, beneath and within the other men, but curiously untouched by them. He felt the spatial power of Chiun behind him, working the Golden Circle of Sinanju. Remo reached out a hand and found a guard's belly at the end of it. The guard whooshed out an explosion of air and found death before he dropped.

The only sounds on the patio were the muffled curses and grunts of the guards and the heavy metallic tinging as their steel weapons were knocked from their hands and hit the stone.

There were only three guards still standing. All were without weapons and in that brief instant of lucidity that sometimes comes in the middle of great stress, they saw that they were being systematically slaughtered. The three turned and ran. Two of them never made it from the patio before they were clipped from behind, at neck level, by Remo and Chiun's feet. The last sound each heard was the cracking of their spinal columns.

The last survivor, the burly square-built guard, was running away down the railroad tracks. Remo and Chiun looked around and Remo saw a power switch on a panel next to the entrance of the house. He pushed it up into the "on" position. Beneath his feet, he could hear the start-up whirring of a powerful generator.

Chiun bent down and picked up one of the heavy automatics. He held it by the barrel end, then with a backhand flip, let it fly. Like a boomerang it soared from his fingertips, out on a line parallel to the railroad tracks. Quickly, it was out in front of the fleeing guard, then slowly, it described a banana-shaped arc in the air, turned back, and swooped down on the guard like an eagle diving from the sky on a hapless rabbit. The spinning gun buried itself deep in the guard's throat. The force of the impact stopped his running and lifted him off his feet, dumping him onto his back. In his final throes, his body revolved. His hand, flung out over his head, touched the third rail from which the rail cars got their electric power. The man's body sparked and sizzled. It twitched along the ground until one involuntary movement broke it free from its electrical connection and it lay still and incinerated between the two lines of tracks.

"Good shot," Remo said.

"Thank you," Chiun said. "Where is the woman?"

They saw the open patio doors and raced toward them.

Jessica Lester found Bobby Jack Billings in a second-floor room.

She had heard voices while standing in the hall and she withdrew her .22 caliber pistol from the holster on her calf. She paused outside a heavy door for a moment, took a deep breath, then pushed the door open and stepped inside.

"Hiya, little black girl. Have a beer."

Bobby Jack Billings looked at her and smiled. He was sitting in his skivvy shorts and a ragged tee shirt on an antique upholstered armchair. The chair was darkened by beer stains. The Oriental carpet around the chair was littered with empty cans. Billings had a small insipid smile on his face as he waved his beer can at the woman.

There was another man in the room. He wore a brocade bathrobe over silk pajamas. The man's hair was jet black and his skin bore the signs of massage and expensive care. He could have been any age from forty to sixty. He was sitting in a chair facing Bobby Jack's. On the delicate hand-carved end table by his right side was a small fluted glass of sherry.

He looked up at Jessica and said, "Just who are you and what do you want here?"

"Mr. Slimone, I presume."

"You presumes right, girl," Bobby Jack said. "My old buddy, Earl Slimone. I'd introduce you right but I don't know your name."

"Name's not important," Jessica said. "I've come to rescue you."

Billings laughed. Slimone suppressed a slight smile. "Rescue him from what, my dear?"

"Don't play dumb," Jessica said. "It's not becoming."

"But I mean it. Rescue him from what? Mr. Billings has been my house guest for a week."

"Thass right," Billings said. "Me and my good old buddy, Earl here, we been hanging out together."

Through her black makeup, Jessica's face showed momentary confusion. Just then Remo and Chiun moved soundlessly past her into the room. Remo looked around.

Chiun said, "Which one is this Billings?"

"The one with the beer can," Remo said. "Come on, Bobby Jack. You're going home." He turned to Jessica. "We'll take over from here."

"Not quite so fast," Jessica said, "I've got a fee involved here."

"I don't think you ought to be greedy," Remo said. "We pulled your bacon off the stove once tonight. Why don't you count yourself lucky and go home?"

"Yeah. Go home," Billings said thickly. "Don't

want a beer, you can go home. Don't like niggers visiting anyway." His face brightened as he focused his eyes on Remo and Chiun. "You'uns want a beer?"

"Shut up," Remo said. He told Jessica, "Put that gun away before somebody gets hurt."

"Perhaps I can make some sense with you," Slimone told Remo. "Just who is this woman? And why is she pointing that gun at us?"

"She's just your friendly neighborhood spy," Remo said. "Don't pay her any mind."

Jessica leaned close to Remo's ear. "Remo," she said. "There hasn't been any kidnapping here. Look at him. Does he look like a prisoner?"

"Then what the hell's he doing here?" Even as he asked the question, he had the answer in his mind.

"You two put this together to dodge the grand jury that's looking into campaign financing, didn't you?" he said.

"Right. Right. Right," said Bobby Jack. "Damn grand juries . . . make you crazy . . . getting so nobody can make a buck anymore without somebody butting in."

"And PLOTZ? And those medals at the train station? Just tricks to muddy up the trail?" Remo asked.

Slimone said sharply, "Bobby Jack, hold your tongue."

Remo shook his head. He would let Smith sort all this out. What he wanted to do now was get out of here with Billings in tow. He decided to take Slimone for good measure.

"All right, you two, on your feet." He looked at Jessica again. "I told you to put that gun away."

She nodded but kept the pistol in her hand.

Slimone stood up. He was a tall thin man and he carried himself straight, with his shoulders back. Bobby Jack tried to crawl up from his seat. On the third try he made it. Remo walked behind them and hustled them toward the door. As he was leaving the room, Bobby Jack made a swipe toward a can of beer which stood on a leather-topped table and chortled when he caught it on the first try. As they were walking down the steps, Slimone and Bobby Jack in front, followed by Jessica, Remo and Chiun, Billings popped the top of the can open and halted the caravan for a moment while he took a long swig of beer.

"Good," he said. "Nothing like a beer when you're dry."

The procession halted momentarily as Slimone stopped in shock when he saw the bodies of his guards on the flagstone patio outside the rear of the house.

"C'mon, let's go," Remo growled. He turned to Jessica who still held her small .22 in her hand. "I told you to put that away."

Just as he spoke, Slimone dove forward onto the patio. His hand reached out and caught one of the fallen guard's .45 automatics. He rolled over and came up with the weapon pointing at the four others. Jessica saw him and jumped out in front of Remo, raising her gun to shoulder height.

She and Slimone fired together. Her bullet caught him full in the face. The slug from his weapon ripped into her heart. Both of them fell.

Remo knelt alongside Jessica but Chiun tapped him on the shoulder and raised him to his feet.

"There is no hope, my son," Chiun said. As Remo looked down at her, then over at Slimone, he saw that both were dead.

So did Bobby Jack Billings. He took another sip of his beer. "Hot damn," he said. "That's good. Now what you say we get out of here?"

"Your friend just got killed and that's all you have to say?" Remo asked.

"Hell with him," Billings said. "Dead's dead. Nothing I can do about that. And anyway, with him dead, I can go back. No grand jury can find out nothing I did wrong without him around. And I don't even know her. Hell with her. Serves the nigger right."

He drank some more from his beer. "I gotta tap a kidney," he said.

"One thing," Remo said. "Did the president know where you were?"

"That peckerhead? I don't tell him nothing. None of his business what I do."

"He was worried about you," Remo said.

Bobby Jack Billings blinked his eyes as if it took an act of will to focus them. "That's his problem," he said. "Now I gotta make wee-wee."

He started off for the side of the house. Remo looked at Chiun, who shrugged.

"You're not going over there, are you?" Remo asked.

"Why not?" Bobby Jack said. He turned as he talked to Remo and swayed from left foot to right foot as if he were a flamingo trying to decide between them. His legs were thin and paste-colored.

"C'mon," Remo said, his face wrinkling in disgust. "Not against the house. Go somewhere else." He waved toward the railroad tracks. "Go over there."

"Make up your mind or I'll go in my skivvies," Billings said. He started to walk off down the railroad tracks. Thirty feet from the house, he stopped between the twin silver rails and yelled back sarcastically, "Is *this* all right?"

"Fine," Remo said.

"Well, thank you very much," Bobby Jack said.

Remo watched as Bobby Jack struggled with the front of his boxer shorts. He turned his back to Remo and aimed himself toward the third rail. Remo turned to Chiun, about to say something, when he heard a crackling sound behind him and spun back.

Bobby Jack had succumbed to his last call of nature. The electric current from the third rail had raced its way up the stream of water from his body and poured into his body. The can of beer in his hand was giving off blue sparks. Billings fell forward across the third rail, where he sputtered once more.

Back on the patio, Remo tossed the switch, cutting off the electric power to the third rail.

"I forgot it was on," he mumbled.

Chiun snickered.

As Remo turned and looked at Bobby Jack's body, he folded his arms stolidly.

"A lot of people got killed because of that nit," Remo said to Chiun.

"That's life," Chiun said.

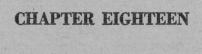

CHAPTER EIGHTEEN

Dr. Harold W. Smith took care of the details. The bodies were removed and it was finally announced to the press that Bobby Jack Billings and his good friend, Earl Slimone, had been accidentally electrocuted on Slimone's Newport estate, where Billings had been visiting for the past week.

Mustafa Kaffir was advised that he was *persona non grata* in the United States and requested to leave within a week.

Smith thanked Remo for his work and said that he felt much better knowing that the president had not ordered the kidnapping of Bobby Jack Billings in an effort to protect himself from an investigation of campaign financing. And, he said, under no circumstances could either Remo or Chiun have permission to compete in the 1980 Olympic games. Under *no* circumstances.

When he hung up the telephone and relayed Smith's message to Chiun, Remo said, "You know, annoying Smitty is the only thing that makes the idea worthwhile."

Chiun said, "Keep thinking that way."

The Number 1 hit man loose in the Mafia jungle . . . nothing and nobody can stop him from wiping out the Mob!

the EXECUTIONER
by Don Pendleton

The Executioner *is without question the best-selling action/ adventure series being published today. American readers have bought more than twenty million copies of the more than thirty volumes published to date. Readers in England, France, Germany, Japan, and a dozen other countries have also become fans of Don Pendleton's peerless hero. Mack Bolan's relentless one-man war against the Mafia, and Pendleton's unique way of mixing authenticity, the psychology of the mission, and a bloody good story, crosses all language barriers and social levels. Law enforcement officers, business executives, college students, housewives, anyone searching for a fast-moving adventure tale, all love Bolan. It isn't just the realism and violence, it certainly isn't blatant sex; it is our guess that there is a "mystique"—if you will—that captures these readers, an indefinable something that builds an identification with the hero and a loyalty to the author. It must be good, it must be better than the others to have lasted since 1969, when* War Against the Mafia, *the first* Executioner *volume, was published as the very first book to be printed by a newly born company called Pinnacle Books. More than just lasting, however—as erstwhile competitors, imitators, and ripoffs died or disappeared—The Executioner has continued to grow into an international publishing phenomenon. The following are some insights into the author and his hero . . . but do dare to read any one of* The Executioner *stories, for, more than anything else, Mack Bolan himself will convince you of his pertinence and popularity.*

The familiar Don Pendleton byline on millions of copies of Mack Bolan's hard-hitting adventures isn't a pen name for a team of writers or some ghostly hack. Pendleton's for real . . . and then some.

He had written about thirty books before he wrote the first book in *The Executioner* series. That was the start of what has now become America's hottest action series since the heyday of James Bond. With thirty-four volumes complete published in the series and four more on the drawing board, Don has little time for writing anything but *Executioner* books, answering fan mail, and autographing royalty checks.

Don completes each book in about six weeks. At the same time, he is gathering and directing the research for his next books. In addition to being a helluva storyteller, and military tactics expert, Don can just as easily speak or write about metaphysics and man's relationship to the universe.

A much-decorated veteran of World War II, Don saw action in the North Atlantic U-boat wars, the invasion of North Africa, and the assaults on Iwo Jima and Okinawa. He later led a team of naval scouts who landed in Tokyo preparatory to the Japanese surrender. As if that weren't enough, he went back for more in Korea, too!

Before turning to full-time duty at the typewriter, Don held positions as a railroad telegrapher, air traffic controller, aeronautical systems engineer, and even had a hand in the early ICBM and Moonshot programs.

He's the father of six and now makes his home in a small town in Indiana. He does his writing amidst a unique collection of weapons, photos, and books.

Most days it's just Don, his typewriter, and his dog (a German Shepherd/St. Bernard who hates strangers) sharing long hours with Mack Bolan and his relentless battle against the Mafia.

Despite little notice by literary critics, the Executioner has quietly taken his position as one of the better known, best understood, and most provocative heroes of contemporary literature—primarily through word-of-mouth advertising on the part of pleased readers.

According to Pendleton, "His saga has become identified in the minds of millions of readers as evidence (or, at least, as hope) that life is something more than some silly progression of charades through which we all drift, willy-nilly—but is a meaningful and exhilarating adventure that we all share, and to which every man and woman, regardless of situation, may contribute some meaningful dimension. Bolan is therefore considerably more than 'a light read' or momentary diversion. To the millions who expectantly 'watch' him through adventure after adventure, he has become a symbol of the revolt of institutionalized man. He is a guy *doing something*—responding to the call of his own conscience—making his presence felt in a positive sense—realizing the full potential of his own vast humanity and excellence. We are all Mack Bolan, male and female, young and old, black and white and all the shades between; down in our secret heart of hearts, where we really live, we dig the guy because *we are* the guy!

The extensive research into locale and Mafia operations that make *The Executioner* novels so lifelike and believable is always completed before the actual writing begins.

"I absorb everything I can about a particular locality, and the story sort of flows out of that. Once it starts flowing, the research phase, which may be from a couple of days to a couple of weeks, is over. I don't force the flow. Once it starts, it's all I can do to hang on."

How much of the Bolan philosophy is Don Pendleton's?

"His philosophy *is* my own," the writer insists. "Mack Bolan's struggle is a personification of the struggle of collective mankind from the dawn of time. More than that, even Bolan is a statement of the life principle—*all* life. His killing, and the motives and methods involved, is actually a consecration of the life principle. He is proclaiming, in effect, that life is meaningful, that the world is important, that it does matter what happens here, that universal goals are being shaped on this cosmic cinder called earth. That's a heroic idea. Bolan is championing the idea. That's what a hero is. Can you imagine a guy like Bolan standing calmly on the sidelines, watching without interest while a young woman is mugged and raped? The guy cares. He is reacting to a destructive principle inherent in the human situation; he's fighting it. The whole world is Bolan's family. He cares about it, and he feels that what happens to it is tremendously important. The goons have rushed in waving guns, intent on raping, looting, pillaging, destroying. And he is blowing their damned heads off, period, end of philosophy. I believe that most of *The Executioner* fans recognize and understand this rationale."

With every title in the series constantly in print and no end in sight, it seems obvious that the rapport between Don Pendleton and his legion of readers is better than ever and that the author, like his hero, has no intention of slowing down or of compromising the artistic or philosophical code of integrity that has seen him through so much.

"I don't go along with the arty, snobbish ideas about literature," he says. "I believe that the mark of good writing can be measured realistically only in terms of public response. Hemingway wrote Hemingway because he was Hemingway. Well, Pendleton writes Pendleton. I don't know any other way."

Right on, Don. Stay hard, guy. And keep those *Executioners* coming!

* * *

[Editors note: for a fascinating and incisive look into *The Executioner* and Don Pendleton, read Pinnacle's *The Executioner's War Book*, available wherever paperbacks are sold.]